Fit To Be Tied

A Southern Quilting Mystery, Volume 11

Elizabeth Craig

Published by Elizabeth Craig, 2019.

FIT TO BE TIED

First edition. August 5, 2019.

Copyright © 2019 Elizabeth Craig.

ISBN: 978-1946227461

Written by Elizabeth Craig.

Chapter One

Beatrice looked around her, feeling a contented warmth as she saw the faces of her quilt guild friends gathered around her daughter. Piper, now about a week out from her due date, was beaming back at them all, a hand resting gently on her large stomach. It was after-hours at the Patchwork Cottage quilt shop, so not only was Beatrice surrounded by friends, she was surrounded by the familiar sights of the shop: bolts of brightly-colored fabric, overstuffed gingham floral sofas, and quilts hanging from the ceiling and draped over every available surface. There was soft music from local bluegrass bands playing in the background.

Meadow, Beatrice's friend and Piper's mother-in-law, leaned over and said, "Isn't this the perfect place for a baby shower for Piper? Where better to introduce our grandchild to quilting?"

"I'm not sure our grandchild is exactly soaking it all in," said Beatrice dryly, as she glanced over at Piper's tummy.

"Sure he or she is! Babies get all sorts of impressions of things in-utero. I've been reading all about it," said Meadow in a firm voice.

Of that, Beatrice had no doubt. Whenever she went over to Meadow's house, there were stacks of baby books everywhere: books on the counters, books on the coffee table, books piled up on the floor. You'd have thought that Meadow was having this baby, herself . . . and being quite proactive in learning about baby care.

Meadow continued, "Babies are completely different now than they were when we had Ash and Piper."

"Are *babies* different? Or is the baby equipment different?" asked Beatrice with a grin.

Meadow chuckled. "You know what I mean. It seems a lot more complicated now than it used to. Why, I remember just putting Ash's baby carrier on the floor of the car and driving around and feeling he was as safe as he could be."

Beatrice reflected that it was a wonder that Meadow's son had survived his formative years.

Everyone from the Village Quilters guild was at the Patchwork Cottage to celebrate the baby's upcoming birth. June Bug, an avid and quiet quilter and owner of a local bakery, had outdone herself with cakes and pastries. There was a caramel cake, a Hershey bar cake, and a sour cream pound cake alongside her homemade doughnuts of different kinds. After liberally tasting a fair number of the offerings, Beatrice was sure that a nap was in her future.

Miss Sissy, the elder stateswoman of the group, growled, "Presents!" The old woman usually was the first to start eating and the last one to stop at any event and her directive made the other guild members stop chatting and blink at her as if the real Miss Sissy had been abducted and someone else put in her place.

"You heard the lady," said Meadow. "Here we are gabbing when we could be giving Piper her presents! And before we tire her completely out. It's been a long time ago, but I still remember how worn-out I used to get when I was carrying Ash."

Piper said, "I've actually been feeling pretty alert! You should see me at the end of the school day, though that's a different story. But I'd love to open presents, if it's time."

Miss Sissy made sure that her gift was the first one that Piper received. Beatrice felt her eyes moisten as Piper reached into a large gift bag holding a beautiful vintage quilt with yellow and white squares. Covering the squares were adorable hand-embroidered ducks, bunnies, frogs, and puppies, all with big, expressive eyes.

Piper gently ran her hand over the quilt. "It's beautiful," she said, eyes shining as she looked at the old woman. "Did your mother make it?"

Miss Sissy nodded abruptly and impatiently rubbed a hand over her eyes.

"I'll make sure we take good care of it," said Piper with a smile.

But Miss Sissy shook her head violently. "Just *use* it," she insisted. "Let baby play on it on the floor."

Piper nodded. "I sure will. It's so soft that the baby will love it."

Miss Sissy looked pleased. "I replaced the batting," she said gruffly.

Piper reached out to give the old woman a hug, and Miss Sissy fiercely hugged her back.

Beatrice gently took the quilt from Piper, gathered it, and carefully folded it up for the return trip to Piper's house and then watched as Piper next picked up a white box with a jaunty yellow ribbon.

"That's from Cork and me," said Posy with a smile.

Piper unwrapped two sets of crib sheets with E.H. Shepard's traditional and much-loved illustrations of Winnie the Pooh scenes covering them.

"Ohhh, I *love* Pooh," said Piper. "And Mama, we forgot to buy sheets."

Beatrice laughed. "In the state we're in Piper, it's amazing we remembered to get the crib itself! I'm not surprised we overlooked them. Thank goodness that Posy had us covered or the poor baby would have been sleeping on something makeshift the first night home."

Savannah, always the pragmatic Village Quilters member, frowned. "There must be some sort of checklist or something online for supplies. I could find one for you and email you."

Piper smiled fondly at her. Savannah was always ready to tackle a challenge and solve a problem. "That would be great. Mama's right—it's like she and I have become super scatter-brained the closer this baby is to coming. I did think of a checklist, but the first one I saw online had a lot of stuff on there that wasn't really *essential*. And the baby won't be tiny forever."

Meadow held up a hand. "Now you stop right there, Piper! This baby hasn't even come yet, and I plan on enjoying every little moment with him or her. You've already got this baby in high school, halfway to the prom!"

Miss Sissy growled at the idea of the baby being in high school. Because her mouth was full of cake, the growl sounded particularly ominous.

Piper gave Beatrice a surreptitious wink. They'd been talking earlier about Meadow's fondness for popping by for visits. Both had the feeling that those surprise visits might be on the rise after her grandchild was born. Although Beatrice acknowledged wryly that *she* might find herself popping over for random visits with Piper, too. Or allegedly with Piper but mainly for the baby.

Savannah said, "And you're *sure* you wanted to be surprised by the baby's gender, Piper? You didn't want to plan for girl or boy toys, or plan the colors for sheets and paint and things?" She frowned. "Or the baby's name?"

"Ash and I thought it would be fun to find out when the baby is born. There aren't so many surprises in life anymore, and we thought this would make for a good one. And there are lots of different options for gender-neutral bedding and toys when the baby is little," said Piper in a soothing voice. Clearly, Savannah would have chosen the path of more planning.

Posy asked, "What are your plans for after the baby arrives, Piper? Are you able to take a little break, or will you be heading back to the classroom right away?"

Piper shook her head. "The timing was really perfect. I'll have the baby soon, in late-spring. Then there will be a substitute teacher for my classroom for the end of the school year. She's perfect since she's a retired teacher who used to teach my grade. Because of all my doctor appointments, the kids have already gotten used to her so it won't be such a hard adjustment. Then there's summer vacation directly after that. I'll feel a lot better about leaving the baby and returning to school when the baby is close to four months old."

Meadow and Beatrice exchanged looks. Meadow was determined to watch the baby, herself, while Piper was at school, although nothing had been said yet. Beatrice had told Meadow that now wasn't really the time to discuss daycare plans since Piper had so much else on her mind with the imminent arrival. There would be time to talk over childcare after the baby's birth.

Georgia, Savannah's sister, said quickly, "I think that's marvelous. Everything is working out so well. I know you're all so thrilled."

Posy asked, "Do you have any pictures of the nursery?"

Piper immediately pulled out her phone and found the photos. "Ash has been working hard in there, although we still have some things to do."

Georgia asked, "Are you enjoying your new house?"

Piper nodded. "It's been fun to have a little more space and a yard. And I love how close we are to town . . . and all of you! We liked our old place too, but the commute was killing us."

The women peered at Piper's phone and all gasped in unison as they looked at the little nursery. There was a comfy armchair with an ottoman in one corner with a small, soft, yellow quilt draped over the chair. There were a couple of shelves on the wall with board books stacked up, including some of Beatrice's favorites: *Goodnight, Moon* and *The Very Hungry Caterpillar*. There was a changing pad on top of a wide chest of drawers. The chest and the crib were both a light gray and the walls were a cheerful yellow.

"It's so sweet," said Georgia.

Savannah, always looking at the practical aspects said, "And it's very practical to put the changing pad on top of the dresser. The diapers and the fresh outfits will all be within reach."

Piper snapped her fingers. "Diaper pail! We've forgotten about that. I mean, I *know* diapers are involved."

"Quite a few of them," said Meadow with a snort.

"And we've already bought some diapers and put them in the chest of drawers. But I totally forgot about the dirty diaper disposal."

Savannah straightened up proudly. "Then you should open *my* present."

Beatrice hid a smile. It was an odd baby shower gift in some ways, but Savannah was excellent at being pragmatic.

Piper laughed. "Perfect! Problem solved."

After the diaper pail had been opened and duly applauded, June Bug handed Piper a small gift.

Piper wrinkled her brow. "But you've already given me your present. The booties and gowns were lovely."

June Bug looked shyly at her. "This is from Katie."

Katie was June Bug's niece. When Katie had lost her mom, June Bug had stepped in to take care of her. It had been a bit of a transition at first, but now Katie was doing well at school, had made friends, and was even doing some quilting.

Piper took the box, which appeared to be carefully wrapped by Katie, using a good deal of tape and the comics section of the last Sunday newspaper. She opened it to see a well-loved stuffed animal—a kitten with big eyes and a plaid bow-tie around his neck. Piper blinked a little as tears filled her eyes.

June Bug said, "It was her favorite toy, but now she's ready to pass it on. Katie wanted the baby to have it."

"Is she sure? This kitten looks like it's had a whole lot of love from Katie," said Piper slowly, running her fingers over the worn cat. "This must be a really special toy."

June Bug nodded, smiling shyly. "She's getting into other toys now. Barbies and things. But she loved that little cat."

"I can see that. Tell her that we'll treasure it like she did—and thanks!" Piper carefully put the kitten with her other presents.

By the end (and after Meadow's and Beatrice's gifts), Piper had accumulated a lot of needed things for the new baby, including a swing, a car seat, and a high chair.

"I never realized how much equipment these tiny little people needed," said Piper, glancing around her.

Beatrice said, "These things will make life easier, for sure. I remember how helpful the swing was for you when you were a baby. You used to fall right to sleep in it while I was putting away laundry or cooking supper."

Piper said in a teasing voice, "So who loved the swing more? You or me?"

"I think it might have been a tie," said Beatrice with a smile.

After the presents were all unwrapped, everyone chatted for a few minutes before the shower wrapped up.

Georgia walked up to Beatrice, her pretty face beaming. "You must be getting so excited."

"It's hard to think of anything else, honestly. Although I really need to be," said Beatrice with a sigh.

Georgia laughed. "How is your home improvement project going?"

Meadow, overhearing her, joined them. "Can you believe it? Who takes on a home improvement project when life is already nuts?"

Beatrice sighed. "It was one of those things that I suddenly just *had* to do. It started out with some minor water damage and a bit of rotted wood. Then I figured that it was a good time to update and remodel since a contractor was already going to have to go in and tear things out. The kitchen cabinets were ancient and needed to be replaced when I moved in, but I procrastinated getting them taken care of."

Georgia said sympathetically, "Sure you did. No one likes taking on a project like that, especially when you're already overwhelmed by moving into a new house."

"In a new town," added Meadow.

Beatrice said, "But then things got worse when Wyatt and I didn't notice that the pipe under the kitchen sink was leaking. We ended up with a fair amount of water damage. I couldn't stand looking at it a moment longer so Wyatt and I started talking to contractors about replacing the cabinets."

Meadow said, "Except that Wyatt is too easy-going and just wants whatever Beatrice wants in terms of new cabinets."

"Can you *be* too easy-going?" mused Georgia.

Beatrice said, "Well, it's a great trait to have and very fitting for a minister. But I really needed some direction. The options for the new cabinetry were completely overwhelming. I had no idea that there could be so many different choices for a small kitchen. And it's a *small* kitchen."

Meadow said, "But it has everything you need, right?"

"Considering the fact that I'm not a fan of cooking, it's just the right size. Anyway, I finally reached a decision and we had Jake to help us with the work—he was highly recommended by a bunch of different people we know in church."

Georgia said, "Oh, I know Jake. He's a friend of Tony's." She frowned. "Actually, I think Tony told me that Jake was having some family issues, isn't he? I was going to see if I could bring food by."

Beatrice nodded. "Unfortunately, he is. His mom isn't doing well, and he's taking care of her until he can figure out if she needs to move to a senior living community. But there's no need to bring over food—his mother lives in Indiana."

"Yikes," said Georgia.

Beatrice nodded. "I really wanted to be able to have him finish the job, but he told me he appreciated the thought but couldn't leave me hanging like that. He doesn't know how long he's going to be in Indiana, but it doesn't sound like a brief trip."

Meadow said, "But the cabinets were halfway ripped out." She shook her head and gave a little laugh.

"Every place and every independent contractor that was recommended to us were all totally booked and couldn't take on an immediate job," said Beatrice.

Georgia winced. "So, what did you do?"

Beatrice said sadly, "We took on someone who was available, considering the kitchen was half-gutted. But he's new to the job, and he's taking a long time. And not necessarily showing up when he says that he is, either."

Meadow's eyes widened. "Did you just give him a key, then?"

"We just didn't feel comfortable doing that because we don't know him at all, and he wasn't recommended by anyone we know. He seems like a nice guy, but he's basically a complete stranger. No, the way it's been working is that he shows up at the house unexpectedly, and I change my plans and hang out there instead. Or he shows up unexpectedly, and I'm *not* at home and have to hurry over there to let him in. Obviously, he's not at the house now, and I'd just tell him it wasn't a good time if he'd called me while I'd been at my daughter's baby shower. But it's pretty inconvenient."

Georgia asked, "How is Noo-noo handling all this?"

Meadow chuckled. "I'm guessing not very well. That corgi's ears are so big that the sounds of the gutting and hammering must be driving her completely batty."

Beatrice said, "That's exactly right. She's been huddled on top of my feet at the house, totally miserable. But since I've been the point person for this and now that it's the start of a new week, Wyatt said that he'd work at the house this week and give me a break."

"Doesn't the noise bother him, too?" asked Georgia.

"Not so much. He puts his earbuds in and plays jazz music and seems to be able to write sermons, compose Sunday school lessons, and pen emails. The only things we need to trade out over is when he has hospital visits and things like that. We're sharing a calendar for all of that now," said Beatrice. "It's an online one so that we can check it while we're away from the house."

Meadow snapped her fingers. "Why doesn't Noo-noo come stay over at our house? It's a *lot* quieter over there and Boris would love to have a sleepover party!"

Georgia gave Beatrice a look and struggled to hide a smile.

Beatrice knew the truth was that Noo-noo would *not* love to have a sleepover party with Boris, no matter how loud it was at home. Boris was a large dog of indeterminate heritage who didn't appear to share any of the personal space issues that Noo-noo had. Plus, Beatrice was not at all convinced that Meadow's house was much quieter, considering how loud Meadow was. But Meadow made it sound like Noo-noo and Boris were going to have a party with manicures, sugary snacks, and a movie marathon.

She quickly said, "Thanks, Meadow! But I think I'll just take Noo-noo with me as much as possible this week. And have lots of walks."

Posy walked up to join them and overheard the last bits of their conversation. "Why don't you leave Noo-noo with me some? She could be the shop dog and greet customers as they come in."

Beatrice glanced over at Maisie, the Patchwork Cottage store cat, who was sleeping on her back in a sunbeam, completely relaxed and at ease, tail twitching as she dreamed. "I'm not sure Maisie would want that. She must have her own little routine by this point and Noo-noo would mess that up."

Posy said, "Oh, Maisie is incredibly laid-back for a cat. Besides, there are plenty of sunbeams here to share with Noo-noo. You know Iris Simpson? She comes in here holding her Yorkie all the time. He's the cutest little thing and has these bright, button eyes. She always puts J.T. down so she can shop, and he trots right over to Maisie. Maisie then proceeds to give him a bath. He even lowers his head so that she can better reach different spots!"

Beatrice chuckled. "You're kidding. Really?"

"Maybe Maisie thinks he's a kitten since J.T. is so tiny," offered Georgia.

Posy said, "She's just completely unfazed. But if you're worried about it, bring Noo-noo over on a leash, and let's see how things go."

Beatrice gave her a grateful smile. "Thanks. Let's do that. I think Noo-noo would be on her best behavior and so grateful to be elsewhere. I do feel bad for the poor dog being stuck inside with all that racket."

Chapter Two

A few minutes later, a few of the guests started trickling out with Piper hugging each one in turn. Miss Sissy left, too, with a paper plate filled with leftover shower food to take home with her. Beatrice helped Piper put her gifts in Beatrice's car.

Beatrice looked at her watch. "I guess we can head out. We should have given Miss Sissy enough of a head-start so that we won't run into her on the road. She's such a hazard that I try not to drive at the same time if I can help it."

Piper gave a big yawn as Beatrice backed the car up and started the trip to Piper's house. Piper said, "It's a good thing you're driving. Like I told everyone, I've been feeling really alert and haven't been tired much. But for some reason, I'm exhausted now. And it was such a fun party for the baby."

Beatrice said, "Well, *I'm* tired and I'm not even expecting! It was a lot of fun, though and good to catch up with everyone, since it's been especially busy lately. What's Ash been up to while we've had the shower?"

Piper chuckled. "Ash is nesting just as much as I am! My theory is that it simply goes unnoticed and uncommented on in men. He's been doing lots of yard work. He's trying to subdue nature," she said fondly.

"Is it working?" asked Beatrice with a smile.

"We'll have to see. There's this natural area in the backyard where he wanted to put a swing-set. When I left, he was out there pulling vines and weeds and hacking away at a thorny bush with a hedge-trimmer." Then she said, "Oh, I forgot. Would you mind going with me to my doctor appointment tomorrow morning? Ash usually goes but he can't make it tomorrow because of something going on at the college."

"Of course, I'll be there," said Beatrice. "How about if I pick you up and we go to lunch afterward?"

"Perfect," said Piper as Beatrice pulled into her driveway.

After Beatrice helped Piper bring her gifts in and spoke to Ash, who indeed had subdued nature, with the impressive results of a stack of yard waste at the side of the road, she drove back home, entering her driveway warily in case a work truck was there. She breathed a sigh of relief and then muttered to herself, "You're supposed to be *glad* to see the workman! The kitchen is totally unusable." Still, it would be nice to sit in the quiet of the house for a little while after the bustle of the shower.

Noo-noo's face popped up in the large picture window at the front of the house, and her intelligent eyes gleamed as she spotted Beatrice. She trotted over to the front door as Beatrice opened it and stooped down to pet the little dog. She opened her mouth and lolled her tongue in a grin.

"Time to eat," she said softly. The corgi erupted with excitement, prancing around her food bowl while Beatrice got out the kibbles.

After feeding Noo-noo, Beatrice poured herself a small glass of white wine and wandered out to the backyard hammock. This was one of her favorite times of day as the sun started setting. The birds were flying between the different feeders that Posy's husband, Cork, had made for her and then flying back to various trees and bushes spotting the yard. She grew sleepy as she counted the cardinals, finches, chickadees, mockingbirds, and woodpeckers, listening to their songs as she drifted off.

She woke with a start as the door leading to the backyard opened. Her husband, Wyatt, said quickly, "Sorry, it's just me. And Noo-noo."

Beatrice made room for him in the hammock and rubbed her eyes with one hand, her other still holding the wine glass. "Wow. I realized that I was getting sleepy when I was listening to the birds, but I had no idea that I'd actually fallen asleep."

Wyatt climbed into the hammock with a chuckle as Noo-noo happily found a soft spot in the lawn to curl up on. "Am I going to break this thing? It's been a little while since we both were in it."

"I don't hear the hammock groaning," said Beatrice.

For a few moments, they were quiet, listening to the wind through the trees, the rustling of leaves, and the contented chirps of birds at the feeders.

Wyatt asked, "How did the shower go?"

Beatrice said, "It was perfect. I'm so glad that Posy offered to host it at the shop. It was so much fun being in there with the guild and surrounded by those gorgeous quilts. Besides, it's always been a special place for Piper, and it was more meaningful for her that the shower was there rather than at a restaurant.

Piper received some really wonderful gifts for the baby, too. And a marvelous vintage baby quilt from Miss Sissy. I'll have to show it to you."

"Sounds like the perfect day," said Wyatt.

Beatrice frowned. "Yes. Well, except for the fact that absolutely nothing got done today in terms of the kitchen project. I sure hope he's going to show up tomorrow."

"Which brings the question: what are we going to do about supper tonight?" asked Wyatt.

"Remind me again what stage of construction we're in? I've lost track. Can we cook on the stovetop? Is the oven plugged in? I haven't even wanted to look because it gives me the most tremendous headache in its current stage."

Wyatt said gently, "I think we're in the frozen waffle stage of renovation. Anything that we can heat up in the toaster should be fine. Or we can eat cold foods from the fridge."

"The fridge that's in our living room?" asked Beatrice with a snort.

"The very one. But we can have yogurt and sandwiches with grapes, if we want. On paper plates, since the dishwasher is disconnected. Or I can run out and pick something up for us," said Wyatt.

"Oh, let's not do that. You've been out all day, and it's too much bother. Besides, I ate a ton at the shower; that's probably why I conked out here in the hammock. Let's have sandwiches, and I'll call to firmly say we need some progress on our project tomorrow. We can't camp out in our own home forever. It gets old, fast."

Wyatt put a foot down and set the hammock to lazy swaying. "That would be perfect. I'm not too hungry, myself. And thanks for calling Dale tomorrow. I'd do it myself, except I'm supposed to have a morning meeting with Gerald Carpenter at his office. He's apparently always up early and requested to meet with me before work. I guess he likes to knock out personal or church business before he really starts his day. Then I'll be back home to monitor the progress on the kitchen so that you can take Noo-noo out of here if you want."

Beatrice groaned. "I'm afraid I'm going to inflict more anxiety on poor Noo-noo. I told Piper that I'd go to her appointment with her tomorrow. It's a noon appointment, and we're going to a late lunch after that." She paused. "Posy did offer to take Noo-noo, although I didn't really think there'd be any need to."

"Take her?" asked Wyatt in a distracted voice.

"Sorry. I meant watch her for me at the shop. I wasn't sure how Noo-noo would do with Maisie the cat, but Posy said that Maisie is very laid-back around dogs. There was talk of Maisie grooming a Yorkie. Maybe I'll drop Noo-noo by there before picking up Piper," said Beatrice. "I'll call her in a little bit and set it all up. What's your meeting with Gerald about tomorrow?"

Wyatt laughed ruefully. "It seems like our entire life is wrapped up in renovations right now. Gerald is doing some of the footwork for me and is getting bids or quotes or something for the HVAC renovation that the church is planning."

"That's going to be a big project," said Beatrice.

"Yes. But the church has put off replacing the heating and cooling systems in the Sunday school building for a long time, so it really has reached a boiling point now," said Wyatt with a sigh.

"No pun intended, right?" asked Beatrice.

"Exactly. Anyway, I'll meet with Gerald and maybe Dale will be ready to work by the time that meeting is over with. I think if Dale has a full day here at the house that he'll be able to make some swift progress," said Wyatt.

Beatrice gave a wry smile. Her husband was always an optimist.

Beatrice woke early the next morning and slipped out of bed while Wyatt was still sleeping. Noo-noo grinned a corgi grin at her as she took her out early for a short walk and then gave her an early breakfast.

She ran out to pick up some fresh-made muffins from June Bug's shop, since it seemed the baked goods Beatrice enjoyed yesterday had just whetted her appetite for more. When she arrived home, Wyatt was already moving around.

He gave her a grateful look as he took one of the muffins she offered him. "Thanks. I'm running just a little late."

Beatrice quirked an eyebrow. "I had no idea you meant that your meeting was *this* early. I thought you meant more like nine o'clock."

"Afraid not. But I'll be out of here in a jiffy. Gerald is something of a stickler with his schedule. Sometimes he's been in charge of meetings at the church and is not the most patient person if someone shows up late."

Beatrice said, "Here, then take another muffin to go and eat it in the car. I'll call Dale and see if he can come over."

Wyatt rushed out with the extra muffin, and Beatrice watched him go out the window as Dale's phone rang and rang. She finally sighed and left a message for him.

Noo-noo looked up at Beatrice in concern, and she rubbed her. "It's terrible to have one's kitchen held hostage by a workman, Noo-noo."

Noo-noo gazed sympathetically at her. Although Noo-noo, of course, had no desire to have the kitchen completed whatsoever. It was a process entirely too noisy for her large ears.

When Beatrice's phone rang fifteen minutes later, she fumbled, relieved, to answer it. She frowned when she saw it was Wyatt and not her contractor.

"Everything all right?" she asked quickly as she answered the phone.

Wyatt's voice was hoarse. "Afraid not. Gerald is dead. And I think he's been murdered."

Chapter Three

Wyatt had already called Ramsay, Meadow's husband and the chief of police in Dappled Hills. By the time Beatrice reached Gerald's business, a factory that manufactured pimento cheese, named Dappled Hills Pimento Cheese, Ramsay was already grimly cordoning off the business so that any arriving employees wouldn't disturb the crime scene.

Wyatt was pale and looked shaken. He gave Beatrice a hug as she approached.

"That must have been awful," she said, squeezing him tightly.

"It was. It was just the unexpectedness of it. The fact that I was going in for a meeting and then, *this*." His face was drawn.

"And you said it didn't appear that Gerald's death was natural?" asked Beatrice.

He shook his head. "No. I mean, I didn't see exactly what could have killed him. He wasn't bloody, and there wasn't a weapon nearby that I could see. But he'd been . . . tied up," he said a bit shakily.

"Tied up?"

"To his office chair. Obviously, there was no way that he could have done that himself," said Wyatt.

Ramsay came back out to them and sighed. "What a way to start a day. I have the state police on the way out here, but I wanted to get a statement from Wyatt first." He hesitated and then said, "Wyatt, you know I don't think you have anything whatsoever to do with this, but I have to ask you some questions. And the state police may, too. It's just that you were the first on the scene here. What were you doing before you came out here?"

Wyatt said ruefully, "Sleeping. Oversleeping."

"Indeed he was," said Beatrice. "He was scrambling to get here on time to meet with Gerald."

"You were together before he drove out?" asked Ramsay, jotting down notes.

Wyatt quickly said, "Beatrice left to pick up muffins for a while."

Beatrice raised her eyebrows. "Maybe for ten minutes, round-trip, from our house to June Bug's bakery. I hardly think you could have driven down here, murdered poor Gerald, and then ended up back at the house to get ready in that amount of time."

Ramsay said, "Neither do I. What were y'all meeting about, by the way?"

Wyatt said, "It was about the church renovation project." When Ramsay frowned, Wyatt continued. "We're putting a new HVAC system into the Sunday school building. Gerald was in charge of hearing quotes . . . I suppose it was more like bids, since it's a big project. He was to report back to me this morning."

Ramsay nodded and jotted down a few notes. "Was Gerald very involved in the church?"

"He was. He was an elder, actually. And he had good business acumen. When he offered to oversee the bids, I was happy to let him take it over."

"Was the door locked or unlocked when you arrived?" asked Ramsay.

Wyatt considered this. He said slowly, "At first, I just knocked. I saw Gerald's car here, and I thought it would be better to knock since it was his office and not a public place. When I didn't get an answer, I thought maybe he was on the phone or something and couldn't answer so I tried the door. It opened right up."

Ramsay jotted down more notes and nodded. "All right. Well, this is quite a mess. And Gerald is one of our most prominent citizens, so there's going to be a lot of local attention focused on this case. I'll need to notify the family. And Wyatt, since the family is so involved with the church, I'm sure you'll be busy, too."

Wyatt said slowly, "It was mostly Gerald who was involved, although I saw his wife with him quite often, and sometimes his son. I'll make sure to stop by and visit with them after you've notified the family."

Ramsay said, "Oh, and if you can both keep the method of his death quiet, I'd appreciate it. At least the part about him being tied up."

"Of course," said Wyatt.

Cars had been driving up and been redirected by Ramsay's deputy as they spoke. But one car simply parked farther away instead of leaving. A tall man wearing a crisp white shirt, pressed gray pants, and a red tie walked briskly up to them.

"Mark Carpenter, Gerald's son," said Ramsay in a sad voice. "This is the worst part of the whole job."

Cutting to the chase, Mark quickly said, "What's happening? Ramsay? Wyatt?"

Ramsay said, "Mark, can I have a few words? Maybe over there?" He pointed to a table and chairs under trees that apparently served as an employee break area.

Mark shook his head. "Here is fine, thanks." He was clearly the kind of man who didn't have much patience with formalities or people trying to be sensitive.

Ramsay said, "I have some bad news. I'm very sorry. Your father died sometime early this morning, after he arrived at work. Wyatt discovered him when he arrived."

Mark turned to Wyatt who said gently, "We were supposed to have a meeting this morning on the church renovations."

Mark pressed his lips together and then took a deep, steadying breath. "I see. Was it a heart attack? I always told Dad that he was working too hard. He was the kind of man who never took a vacation and rarely even took breaks during the day."

"I'm afraid his death wasn't natural. We're opening a murder investigation," said Ramsay somberly.

Mark's face was a study of confusion. "Murdered? Dad?" He took a small step back and then stood perfectly still as if to prove that he was fine. "That's quite a shock." But to Beatrice, he seemed more taken aback than truly shocked. But he definitely seemed confused and as if his mind was going in a million directions.

Mark put his hand to his head as if it hurt. "That's going to be terrible for the business."

Beatrice and Ramsay glanced at each other.

Mark continued, "Sorry. That must have sounded very unfeeling. It's actually the first thing that my father would have said if the roles were reversed. Let's see if I can explain. It's just that part of the appeal of the business is the family aspect of it. The social media campaigns that our marketing gal runs and that sort of thing. If you have ever eaten the pimento cheese, you'll know that there's a black-and-white family portrait on the lid of every container. Marketing is centered on the happy family approach. This is going to be hard to gloss over."

Ramsay's brows arched just a little in recognition of Mark's statement then he said, "The state police are on the way. We'll be sure to find out who's responsible for your father's death." The grim way he said it made Beatrice wonder if it was a threat or a promise.

Ramsay added, "Speaking of the family business, how were things going over there? I'd imagine it would be mighty hard to work with family all the time. Business doing okay?"

Mark said briskly in a practiced way, "The business is doing very well. We've had lots of retailers ask to partner with us in selling to the public and we've stepped up our distribution accordingly. We've also had a lot of excellent media coverage lately."

"Was it hard to work with your father?" pressed Ramsay. "It's just that spending all day with someone that you're closely related to can be challenging, I'm sure."

Mark gave him an unwavering, direct look. "Of course not. We were lucky to have the founder of the business so invested in the company and its growth. Dad was good for the company. He was the face of the company and having him around and having the employees see how hard he worked was motivating for everyone who worked for him. Including me."

Ramsay changed tack. "What were you doing this morning?"

Mark shrugged. "Nothing remarkable. Until a few minutes ago, it was about as normal of a day as you could possibly imagine. I took the dog out, showered, dressed, drank coffee, and looked over my schedule. I answered a few emails, ate two eggs for breakfast, brushed my teeth, and hopped into the car. The usual."

Ramsay said, not unkindly, "And your wife can verify all that?"

Mark shook his head. "I've been divorced for the last year. My former wife lives in Florida now." He paused. "Look, what's the plan for today? I need to know what to tell the employees."

Ramsay said smoothly, "I'm afraid the business is going to be closed for the day, likely tomorrow, too. We'll have forensics guys here and other investigators. But we'll get you up and running as soon as we can." He paused and then continued, "It's hard to imagine, but did your father have any enemies? Did he maybe make folks unhappy in the business world? Competitors?"

Mark considered this a second and then shook his head decisively. "No. Dad had lots of peers, instead—fellow businessowners who were growing in their own field. Sometimes he advised other people, especially those who were up and coming or new to owning their own businesses. But there wasn't any sort of competition for him, really, in terms of pimento cheese." Mark's voice ended up on a proud note before he became somber again.

"On a personal side, then?" pressed Ramsay. "Is there anyone whom he'd upset? Someone who held a long-term grudge or who he'd recently made angry?"

Mark didn't have to consider this as long. "Well, you know Dad. He did pretty much whatever he wanted to do. Sometimes he rubbed people the wrong way. He could be blunt, which is a trait that I admire, but I know it could sometimes come across as abrasive. When you asked the question, there was one particular person who did come to mind, although I'm not saying that she had anything to do with it."

"Who is that?" asked Ramsay.

"Her name is Salome Hewitt. She used to work for Dad; actually, she worked for him for many years," said Mark.

Beatrice said slowly, "I know Salome. She's helping Posy part-time at the Patchwork Cottage."

Mark said, "Is she? Well, it's good that she has work somewhere."

Ramsay asked, "What makes her an *ex*-employee? And what are her feelings about your dad or not working for the company any longer?"

Mark sighed. "Dad was a good businessman, but he didn't have a lot of people-skills and he could sometimes be fairly miserly. Salome has a small child and asked Dad for a raise in pay to feed two mouths instead of one. I doubt that she'd had a raise in all the years she'd worked for him, but he fired her instead for her impudence in asking him." He shook his head.

Beatrice and Wyatt glanced at each other.

Ramsay said, "I see. So clearly, she wasn't happy about that. Getting the axe after years of loyal service."

Mark shrugged his shoulders. "I'm sure she was completely shocked. She went into Dad's office expecting a raise and left without a job. Dad told me that there were plenty of people who'd love to have her job. And it didn't take him long to find one of them. Although I don't think he's been nearly as happy with her as he was with Salome. Salome was used to all of Dad's idiosyncrasies and knew how he liked things organized in his office. Dad was always very particular about his files."

Ramsay nodded and closed his notebook. "Thanks for this, Mark. I'll be asking you some more follow-up questions later on, but that's all I have for now." He walked over to greet the state police, who'd just pulled up.

Mark blew out a breath and said to Wyatt, "I'm glad you're here, Wyatt. Could you be sure to reserve the sanctuary for us for Dad's funeral?"

Wyatt said, "Of course I will." He pulled out his phone. "When should I reserve it for?"

Mark said, "One second." He hurried back over to Ramsay and consulted with him and then walked back. "Let's plan for four or five days from now, to be on the safe side. I'll have to check in with Laura, Dad's wife, of course. Do you think there's availability?"

Wyatt peered at the calendar on his phone. "It looks like there is, although I'll check in with Edgenora, our church admin, to make sure."

Mark said, "Thank you. I'll be in touch."

A few minutes later, Wyatt and Beatrice were walking to their cars.

Beatrice saw how quiet Wyatt was and gently said, "That must have been very hard, seeing Gerald like that."

He sighed. "It was. In fact, I think I'm going to head straight home and regroup. I originally thought I might run by the store for more groceries to make for easy meals, but I think I need to sit down."

"I can run by the store after I drop Piper off later. I'll follow you back now, since it's too early to meet up with Piper."

Wyatt nodded absently as he unlocked his car and Beatrice followed him back home, walking into the house behind him as he sat down in the living room.

"What do you make of all that?" he asked Beatrice. "I mean, you've seen Ramsay run investigations before. Do you think he thought Mark had something to do with his father's death?"

Beatrice said slowly, "I think Ramsay is just asking all the questions that he has to ask. The police always say that the most likely culprits are people who are closest to the victim."

"I don't suppose it was some sort of random crime?" asked Wyatt, rubbing his temples.

"It would be nice to think so, wouldn't it? Except it doesn't make any sense. Why would a stranger kill Gerald Carpenter?"

"A theft gone wrong?" asked Wyatt.

Beatrice shook her head. "A factory isn't the kind of place that has money on hand. And Gerald was more of a penny-pincher, remember? He wasn't the sort to have fancy computers and monitors there. No, it's more likely to be a family member or an employee or someone Gerald did business with."

Wyatt said, "Mark mentioned a woman who used to work for Gerald. You know her?"

"I wouldn't say that I *know* Salome, but she's helped check me out when I was buying fabric at the Patchwork Cottage. She seems really sweet and knows a good deal about quilting, too. Posy recently hired her for extra help; I guess Salome must have started working there when she lost her job at the factory." Beatrice added, "It sounds as if Gerald was a tough person to work for."

Wyatt said, "I think he was a tough person altogether. I know that he was used to people doing whatever he wanted them to do, which was why I didn't say anything when he offered to handle the bidding for the air conditioning and heating work. Besides, with all of his business experience, I figured he was a good guy for the job. He was also always incredibly organized and stayed on top of tasks well."

"That's probably why he was able to be so successful when starting his own business," said Beatrice. "People like him are completely driven."

"I forgot to ask whether or not you were able to get hold of Dale about the work," said Wyatt, rubbing his eyes with the palms of his hands as if he was exhausted.

"Oops. No, unfortunately, he didn't answer—and then I ran over to the factory when you called me. I've totally forgotten about the kitchen until now, but I can give him a call." Beatrice pulled out her phone.

"Honestly? I know this is awful, but I think I'd rather deal with eating yogurts out of the living room fridge again than deal with the construction racket today. My head is already pounding. If Dale ends up stopping by, that's fine. But I don't think I want to *try* to get him over here, if that makes sense." He walked back to the bathroom and opened the medicine cabinet for an ibuprofen and then joined Beatrice again. He had a worried expression on his face. "What did you think about Mark?"

Beatrice said, "I don't really know Mark all that well. I mean, I see him at church sometimes, but he's not exactly a regular. I think he was surprised by Gerald's death, but I don't think he was very upset by it. And I might be completely wrong; I know that grief is expressed in different ways by different people."

"That's true. There doesn't seem to be a really standard grief reaction. I thought he seemed stunned, but you're right—I got the impression that he was more concerned by the impact on the business. But maybe that's just his background—always to worry about the business side of things. He does have a lot of employees that are depending on the company to do well and Mark likely feels very responsible toward them." Wyatt sat down again.

Beatrice said, "It makes sense. But it did come off as slightly cold. Maybe he and his father didn't get along very well."

Wyatt said, "It might be that they had a good business partnership but simply didn't have very much in common and weren't all that close."

Beatrice smiled at him. "You always have such a generous mindset toward people."

Wyatt grinned back at her. "As a minister, it's part of the job."

The doorbell rang and Wyatt made a face. Then he chuckled. "Why aren't I in a generous mindset right now?"

Beatrice sighed. "I suppose it's Dale. With any luck, maybe there's a light at the end of the tunnel with this kitchen project. Unless it's the light from an oncoming train."

She opened the door, and Dale stood there with an apologetic expression and his arm in a sling.

"Dale! What on earth happened?" Beatrice ushered Dale inside.

The young man looked abashed. "Well, I somehow managed to fracture my shoulder when I was out four-wheeling with my cousin. I reckon that's the *last* thing you want to hear from me, but it's the truth."

Wyatt said, "If you had an accident on an ATV, you're fortunate that a shoulder fracture is all that happened."

Dale nodded. "Ain't that the truth? My mama always told me not to go four-wheeling with Duane. She never thought he had any sense. And we was lucky the thing didn't flip on top of us. Anyways, I won't be doing that again." He paused and looked at them apologetically. "The doctor says I gotta have this arm in a sling to keep it still and let the bones heal the right way. I'm sorry, y'all. I know you was counting on me to finish up the job."

"If you can't do it, you can't do it," said Beatrice. She looked at Wyatt. "We'll just have to find someone who's available to complete the kitchen."

Dale said, "My cousin does a lot of construction work. Of course, he mostly works for a business, but he's starting to do some stuff on the side."

Beatrice raised her eyebrows. "Not Duane? The four-wheeling free spirit?"

Dale laughed. "Nope. I wouldn't recommend Duane for much of anything. He's kind of reckless. But I have *another* cousin, Len, who knows his way around a kitchen. I can send him out to talk to you this afternoon, if you like. I feel bad about leaving you in a spot."

Wyatt said, "If Len can come by this morning or afternoon, that would be great. I'm going to be here."

Dale gave them Len's contact information and a few more apologies before he left.

Beatrice leaned back against the front door after Dale had gone out of it and closed her eyes. "It's the never-ending project."

"With any luck, maybe Len has some references or can inspire confidence in some way," said Wyatt. "Unfortunately, I think we're starting to run out of options. Whoever is available is probably going to be key."

"I think you're right." Beatrice glanced at her watch. "Okay, it's about time for me to go pick up Piper. Do you want me to drop off Noo-noo at Posy's in case Len comes over and is ready to immediately start?"

Wyatt hesitated, looking at Noo-noo, who had a hopeful expression on her face. "Why not test it out and see how it goes? Maybe it would be better to try a Patchwork Cottage visit in short spurts."

Beatrice nodded. "Good idea. Then I can pick up Noo-noo after Piper and I have lunch and see how it went."

Chapter Four

"Noo-noo," said Posy in a tender voice as the little dog trotted in. Noo-noo wriggled her entire rear end and then flopped over immediately for a tummy rub while grinning lovingly up at Posy.

There were a handful of customers in the Patchwork Cottage, and they all hurried over to ooh and ahh over Noo-noo and then show pictures on their phones of their own dogs.

Posy beamed at Beatrice and said in a low voice, "I think Noo-noo might be a big draw for folks to shop here! She's certainly a conversation-starter." They glanced over at the women who were still sharing pictures with each other and loving on the corgi, who was soaking it all up.

Beatrice said, "If she's not a tremendous distraction! We want them to buy fabric and notions, not pet Noo-noo." She looked fondly at the corgi, who was grinning at everyone as she lay on her back.

Posy laughed. "And look at Maisie! Like I said, I didn't think there would be any issues with our store cat."

Maisie, a large white cat, was trotting toward Noo-noo, weaving around the legs of the customers on her way to see the little dog. Then she observed Noo-noo solemnly before going up to groom Noo-noo's head, which Noo-noo lay very still for.

Beatrice grinned. "I think they've made friends."

The whole shop was chuckling over the two and one woman took pictures with her phone.

Posy said, "Well, I think you can rest assured that Noo-noo will be fine here while you take Piper to her appointment."

"She'll never want to go home!" said Beatrice. "Thanks so much. I'll check in on her after the appointment and before we go to lunch, just to make sure."

Posy shook her head. "Don't worry about it. I'll send you an update in a little over an hour. Regardless, have a nice lunch with Piper! I know y'all will enjoy that."

Piper's appointment went really well. Beatrice's eyes had welled up a few times during the doctor visit, particularly when they heard the baby's heartbeat and saw the baby on the monitor.

"You have a fine baby," said the doctor with a smile at them as she very carefully avoided any gender pronouns that might reveal if the baby was a boy or girl. "And seems very healthy."

Posy did indeed send Beatrice an update, just as she and Piper were making their way out of the doctor's office. In the picture she sent, Noo-noo was grinning obligingly at the camera as Maisie lay curled up against her, blissfully sleeping.

Beatrice showed the photo to Piper as they got into Beatrice's car. Piper snorted. "That is one laid-back cat!"

"Posy thought she'd be completely fine with a dog in the shop, and Maisie was," said Beatrice. She looked over at Piper as she started driving toward downtown. "How are you doing?"

Piper said, "Great! I really haven't had any issues and nothing to complain about. The baby has been really active during the day, which is kind of fun. And at night, he or she seems to conk out and go to sleep, which allows *me* to sleep."

"I have a brilliant grandchild," said Beatrice with a smile.

Piper picked a restaurant right in downtown. It was a pretty place with cheerful pastel murals on the walls and white tablecloths and a single flower in a vase on each table. Even though the ambience made it feel like a special occasion, the pricing was moderate. And the restaurant offered a huge selection of food.

They were about to walk in when Meadow approached them on the sidewalk. "How did the appointment go, Piper?" she asked a bit breathlessly. She followed Piper's appointments religiously and had clearly restrained herself from texting and asking for an update before now.

"Everything is fine," said Piper in a soothing voice. "The baby is doing great."

Meadow's face relaxed immediately. "Wonderful news!" Then she turned to Beatrice and said urgently, "I need to talk to you later. Fill me in!" She gave Piper a hug and said, "So excited!" And she was off again, heading briskly in the direction of the grocery store.

After they ordered,—Piper choosing their chicken salad plate and Beatrice opting for a quiche with a salad—Piper said, "Okay, so what was Meadow alluding to so mysteriously? I can't imagine it's the work you're having done at your house."

Beatrice sighed. "Or the work that's *not* being done at our house." She filled Piper in quickly on losing Dale because of injury and ending up with Dale's cousin, Len. Then she paused. "I think that Meadow was being cautious because she's being protective of you. She doesn't want you to be worried about anything right now."

Piper lifted an eyebrow. "You mean *over*protective. And now my curiosity is definitely piqued. What was it that Meadow was tiptoeing around? Something happened, right? Is everything okay with Wyatt? You're both feeling well?"

Piper had always been intuitive so Beatrice wasn't too surprised when she honed in on Wyatt. Beatrice said, "He's fine, although he had a bit of a shock this morning. I think I mentioned to you that he had a meeting early today."

Piper frowned. "You did, although I can't remember with whom."

"With Gerald Carpenter. He's been in charge of getting bids for that air conditioning and heating project at the church. Unfortunately, when Wyatt arrived, he found Gerald dead."

Piper's eyes opened wide. "Did he have a heart attack or a stroke or something?"

Beatrice shook her head. "No. I'm afraid he was murdered." She sighed. "Even though Wyatt, as a minister, has seen a lot of death, Gerald's murder really seemed to shake him up."

Their waitress served them and then Piper said, "I bet it did. It would have upset anyone and Wyatt can be a real softie. Were there any clues as to who might be responsible?"

"Nothing that Ramsay divulged to us, although the state police's forensics team was there trying to get more information," said Beatrice. "Gerald's son, Mark, arrived and spoke to us for a few minutes."

Piper grimaced. "I'm sure he took it hard. He spent a lot of time with his dad at the business."

Beatrice said, "He definitely seemed surprised. And, of course, everyone processes grief differently, but I didn't get a real sense that he was devastated. He was mostly talking about the business and the employees." She took a bite of her quiche, which melted in her mouth. She wondered why her own quiches always seemed to be tough. Once again, she felt as if she likely didn't possess the patience to be a good cook.

"I don't think he's the kind of person who's really in touch with their emotions," said Piper. "He always has this very tight smile. He seems really high strung to me. And I know he invests a lot of time in the family business. Maybe he'll be dealing with his father's death in a more private way. I don't think he'd give away much emotion in public."

Beatrice said, "I think that Gerald might also have been challenging to work with. He always seemed to like to do things his way, according to Wyatt. That might rub someone like Mark the wrong way since he *also* seems to like to do things his way. I wonder if they had any disagreements over the running of the business."

Piper finished a bite of her chicken salad and then said, "I know someone who probably knows a lot about how Gerald and Mark worked together. Salome Hewitt."

"I remembered Salome works at the Patchwork Cottage now," said Beatrice. "I didn't see her there when I dropped Noo-noo off at the shop."

"Maybe she'll be there when you're picking Noo-noo up. She worked for Gerald a long time and must have all sorts of thoughts on Gerald and Mark and the rest of the family," said Piper.

Beatrice frowned. "I'm guessing they're not great thoughts. Mark mentioned that Salome might have something of a grudge against the family because of the way she was forced out of the company."

"She doesn't seem really happy about it, that's for sure. Posy wanted to give Salome work because she has her preschool-age daughter to care for and didn't have a job at all. Salome was apparently fired really abruptly and fairly recently. And Salome has quilted for years, so she was familiar enough with the business to step right into the job." Piper took a sip of her sweet tea and pushed her empty plate to the side.

Beatrice asked, "Was Salome in a guild?"

Piper shook her head. "With her busy life, she wouldn't have had time to join one."

Beatrice said, "Mark said that Salome was fired because she asked for a raise. Although that seems a little harsh since Salome was apparently an employee of long-standing. Mark also said that Gerald liked the way that Salome kept everything organized. So it seems that she did a good job."

"Right. Salome is pretty bitter over that point. But fortunately, she has some help in town. Her sister lives here, and she's taken her and her daughter, Jenna, in since Salome couldn't afford her apartment anymore. It must be very hard on all of them."

Beatrice felt a little like Meadow as she changed the subject. But she wanted to dwell on some happier topics. "Speaking of homes, how is the indoor-outdoor nesting process going?"

Piper beamed. "It's going well! Better than yours, apparently," she said with a light laugh.

"As long as any sort of progress is being made, your project is going *much* better than mine," said Beatrice.

And for the next thirty minutes, they chatted about nurseries and baby equipment and the new sandbox that Ash had made in their backyard.

Later, Beatrice drove Piper back home, exclaimed over the sandbox and the most recent updates to the nursery, and then drove over to the Patchwork Cottage to pick up Noo-noo . . . and see if Salome Hewitt might be working there.

As it happened, a large number of shoppers had just left the shop, and Salome *was* there, making Beatrice think that maybe Posy's employee had been working in the back room when Beatrice had been there earlier. Posy grinned at Beatrice, "I'm worn out. And I know Salome is."

Salome was a small, attractive woman with shoulder-length black hair and dimples that appeared when she smiled. "That was a lot of checking out at one time."

Posy said, "But it would have been much worse if Noo-noo hadn't been here as a distraction. Then they *all* would have checked out at the same time instead of just half of them. They were all giving Noo-noo attention."

Beatrice said, "I'm sure she absolutely basked in it, too."

Posy said, "She definitely did! She was such a happy dog. Everyone loved seeing her big, doggy smile. Be sure to bring her back anytime. We loved having her here, and Maisie loved her, too." She glanced over at Salome and said, "Could you keep an eye on the shop for me while I catch up on some paperwork and inventory in the back room? I've been meaning to do it and just can't seem to find the time."

"Of course," said Salome.

Posy quickly headed off to the back room of the shop, and Salome said quickly, "Actually, Beatrice, I was hoping for the opportunity to speak with you."

Beatrice noticed that there were weary lines around her mouth and eyes and that Salome seemed tense. "What can I help you with?"

Salome said quietly, "One of the customers who came in was talking about a suspicious death over at the factory—the pimento cheese factory that Gerald Carpenter owns. And she said that your husband had been there. I was wondering if you had any information about what happened. I used to work there, you see, before I started working for Posy."

"I see. Wyatt was there early this morning for a meeting with Gerald—a meeting that didn't happen. I'm afraid that when Wyatt got there, Gerald was dead. And yes, the police are treating his death as suspicious. When Wyatt called me, I drove over to join him there," said Beatrice.

Salome abruptly took a seat in the seating area a few feet away and Beatrice joined her. Noo-noo opened one eye to observe her before quietly falling back asleep.

Salome said under her breath, "I can't believe it. Who would do something like that?" Then she grimaced. "I bet the police will be over to speak to me soon."

"Why is that?" asked Beatrice, hoping that Salome would offer up the entire story so that she wouldn't have to ask.

Salome did seem in the mood to talk. She gushed, "Because of the way I left the company. I'd worked there for ten years and then Gerald fired me really abruptly, and I was scrambling to find work. I have a young daughter, and I didn't know where to go. I was so relieved when Posy offered me some work, even though it's just part-time. So far, it's been working out for me because I've been able to move in with my sister, Carla, and cut back on expenses."

"Why did Gerald fire you?" asked Beatrice.

Salome gave a harsh laugh. "It didn't make any sense at all to me. But I should have known he might react the way that he did. Gerald had always been really tight-fisted with his money. As I mentioned, I'd been at the company for ten years. I was doing all right, but felt as though I was just scraping by and living paycheck to paycheck. Most of my income was going to my rent. On my ten-year anniversary, I used that date as a springboard to ask for a raise. I figured that ten years of loyal service must be worth something. I mean, I was at that company for so long that I *still* have all of Gerald's contacts on my phone, as if he's going to ask me to make a call for him. But, despite all that service, I was so nervous. Maybe, subconsciously, I knew that it wasn't going to go well. I practiced asking for the raise in front of the mirror ten or fifteen times and crafted my language to make sure that I sounded grateful as well as deserving of more income."

"And he fired you for asking?" asked Beatrice.

"Yes. Not only was Gerald tight-fisted, he could also be fairly childish. He saw my request as evidence of my dissatisfaction and lack of loyalty to the company. It made him mad. He thought I should be grateful for the job, and he fired me on the spot." Salome looked at Beatrice and then said slowly, "There's a bit more, too. I hesitate to bring it up, but I need to talk about it with someone. And I've hashed it out with Carla so many times that I think she's tired of hearing about it."

"Of course. I'd be happy to listen," said Beatrice.

"I appreciate that," said Salome with a warm smile. "Also, I'd like for you to share it with Wyatt. If you don't mind, I'd really like to schedule a pastoral visit with him at the church to talk about this. And to talk about how to find forgiveness in my heart. Because right now, I don't have it in me to forgive, and it feels like I have a hole in my soul."

"I'll do that as soon as I get back home. He'll be in touch," said Beatrice.

Salome took a deep breath and glanced around her to make sure the shop was still just as quiet as she thought. "I made a mistake," she said in a low voice. "My child is Gerald's daughter."

Chapter Five

Beatrice carefully kept her gaze level. "I see." Salome still looked ashamed, and Beatrice continued, "It sounds as if you weren't the *only* person to make a mistake."

Salome gave a shaky laugh. "Well, that's certainly true. And I love my daughter so much—I'd do anything to protect her and to make sure that she has a good life. *She* could never be a mistake, but my actions were. But Gerald's reaction was to immediately shun us both when I told him."

Beatrice asked, "You told him during that meeting when he fired you?"

She nodded. "That's right. I hadn't told him the whole time that I was pregnant or for the next three years after Jenna was born."

Beatrice asked slowly, "What made you decide to keep the information to yourself? And not ask for help right away?"

Salome said sadly, "It was my pride. I could see the other employees looking at me at the office when I started to show. I knew what they thought of me. They had no idea that Gerald was my child's father, but they still had a low opinion of me because they knew that I wasn't married. It stung. And when my pride has been stung, I tend to raise my chin and not say a word. I thought I could handle everything by myself." She paused. "And maybe, part of me realized that asking Gerald Carpenter for help was going to end poorly."

"What made you think that?" asked Beatrice.

Salome sighed. "He was a very stingy man in a lot of ways. I think Gerald was good for the grand gesture—every once in a while, he'd go to a swanky charity event and make a sizable donation that would put his name on a building or something. But then he'd go right back to his penny-pinching ways directly afterward."

"That was very brave of you to finally ask him for some help," said Beatrice, smiling at her. "And it sounded as if your raise was long-overdue anyway. By all accounts, you were a great assistant and kept his office exactly the way he wanted it."

"It was hard. But I realized finally that I couldn't really do it all on my own, and it wasn't fair for me to have to struggle every day. But I was so nervous, especially when I told him about Jenna. I pointed out that surely he'd want the same thing for this child that he wanted for his other children—a decent home, a good life. But he was furious and got rid of me right then and there." Maisie, the shop cat, sensing that Salome was distressed, trotted over and jumped in her lap, bumping her head against Salome's shoulder.

"Again, I think it's amazing that you didn't tell him about your daughter long before. When you first knew about her," said Beatrice.

Salome said, "I just couldn't figure out what to do. I knew Gerald, and I was worried that he was going to erupt when he found out. I wondered if maybe he'd think that I was trying to trap him into marriage or something."

Beatrice frowned, trying to remember Gerald's family, one out of all the families in the church. She did still have a hard time trying to remember them all. "He *is* married, isn't he?" There was the distinct possibility that he wasn't, though . . . that he could be divorced, like his son was.

Salome nodded. "That's right. He's married to Laura, and I don't think he had any intention of leaving her. She's his second wife, as you might remember."

Beatrice shook her head. "I didn't realize that. I haven't lived in town for very long, and I'm still learning everyone's backstories."

Salome said, "He was married before—Mark and Joan are his children from his previous marriage. I never had any illusions that Gerald would leave Laura for me, and I wasn't completely sure what his reaction would be when I told him. No one at the office ever asked me who my baby's father was. They just gave me a little time off when she was born, hired a temp, and generally forgot about her. So I didn't say anything for a long time. But it's a struggle making ends meet with another mouth to feed, and I needed to get child care. I felt pressed to ask for a raise."

"Of course you did," said Beatrice. "And it was the responsible thing to do, for the sake of Jenna."

Salome gave her a grateful look. "Thank you. I wouldn't have done it, except for her." She paused. "And there's another thing. I was there this morning."

"This morning? You mean at the factory?" asked Beatrice. She felt her breath catch a little.

Salome took in another deep breath, and Maisie lovingly brushed against her again with a quiet mew. "I'm afraid so. I'll need to tell Ramsay that when he comes to talk to me. That is, if he doesn't already know. My sister had convinced me that I needed to talk to Gerald again. That he did have a financial responsibility to my daughter, regardless of whether I was employed by him or not. She asked me to just keep calm and steady and try and reason with him. Perhaps he wouldn't have the same reaction the second time around. She thought maybe he'd been so shocked at the news that Jenna was his child that it made him angry."

"I think the courts would agree that he had a financial responsibility, too," said Beatrice.

Salome gave her that grateful look again. "I didn't want to be pushy, you know. I just wanted to help him to see some sense. To see that he couldn't simply abandon us and pretend that our daughter didn't exist and not assist at all with her welfare."

Beatrice said, "Did you end up seeing him?"

Salome shook her head. "I drove up into the parking lot, but I didn't see his car. Usually, it was Gerald's habit to get to the office before dawn, so it was unusual for him not to be there. I wanted to catch him before anyone else was there, but it appeared that he hadn't gotten there yet. I waited for a few minutes, but then ended up driving away."

"And you didn't see anyone else there?" asked Beatrice.

Salome glanced away as she shook her head. Then she reached down to rub Maisie under her chin. Beatrice wondered if she'd imagined the split-second of hesitation she'd sensed from Salome.

Beatrice said, "The news must have been a shock to you this morning."

Salome gave a dry laugh. "I felt a chill go up my spine when I heard the customer talking about it. I tried to pretend that everything was normal. That's why I'm so relieved to be telling you about this, Beatrice, seeing as how you're a preacher's wife and everything. And I'll tell Wyatt the same. I've just felt so bad, so guilty about all this."

Beatrice said slowly, "I've heard that Gerald could be a difficult man to be around. That he liked things done his way. Might there have been other suspects for the police to consider? With that type of personality, I can't imagine that you'd be the only person the police would be looking at."

Salome considered this. Then she said, "I hate mentioning this, because it makes it sound like sour grapes. But I'm not the only person that Gerald had an affair with. I didn't realize this at the time because he'd been very good at keeping his private life private. But he'd already moved on to someone else after his brief relationship with me." She made a face. "You must be wondering how I could want to be with a person like Gerald. But he wasn't always like this. He could be kind, as well as harsh."

"Did you get a sense that he'd changed?" asked Beatrice.

Salome nodded in agreement. "Absolutely. I don't know if it was a midlife crisis, or what. But suddenly, he did seem to be different."

Beatrice reflected that Gerald was a bit old to be having a midlife crisis, but she kept her expression neutral.

Salome took a deep breath and said, "There's this woman that he met at a fundraiser in Lenoir. Her name is Colleen Roberts. Apparently, she's really wealthy, and they were both at this event where people were trying to get them to donate to a political cause. She seems to have a really swanky lifestyle and lives in this huge house and has several fancy cars and stuff like that. I think Gerald might have been fascinated by the thought that someone wasn't interested in his money at all. That someone could be interested in just *him*." Salome absently stroked Maisie.

Beatrice said, "And they started seeing each other?" Noo-noo walked sleepily over and Beatrice reached down to pull her up onto her lap. Noo-noo took up all of Beatrice's lap and then some. But the little dog fell right to sleep.

"That's right. Until . . . they didn't. Gerald's daughter, Joan, is a friend of mine, and she's been upset at the way Gerald had been treating me. She knew that he'd fired me because I'd asked him for a raise. I think she also guessed who my daughter's father might be, although I never said a word to her. Anyway, she was *not* happy that her dad was seeing Colleen. Joan had apparently seen them out together when she was in Lenoir and confronted her father about it later."

"And he admitted to his daughter that he was seeing Colleen?" asked Beatrice.

"That's what she told me. He told her that he was trying to keep the affair quiet, and Joan told him that he wasn't doing a good job if his own daughter was able to find out about it. I mean, Joan is no fan of Gerald's wife, Laura, but I think she felt as if Gerald was really taking things too far."

Beatrice asked, "Because he was having several affairs?"

"She complained to me that he was really behaving badly. And then, the next thing we knew, he broke up with Colleen. He does get tired of people and sort of tosses them to the side." Amazingly, Salome said this without rancor. "And I guess that's what happened with Colleen."

Beatrice asked, "Was it a mutual breakup? Or might Colleen be harboring some bad feelings for Gerald?"

Salome snorted. "Oh, I think she's definitely harboring bad feelings. Joan said that Gerald had the insane idea to break up with her in a public place. A restaurant in Lenoir, Joan told me. I suppose he thought that would be a good way to prevent any hysteria or arguments. But apparently, Colleen didn't care a whit whether they were in a public place or not. Joan said that Colleen really flipped out. She started yelling at Gerald. Practically foaming at the mouth. I think Gerald was shocked." This made Salome smile a little at the thought.

Beatrice said, "Well, if she's a wealthy woman, sometimes with wealth comes a feeling of entitlement. Maybe she wasn't used to being broken up with. Perhaps she usually got her way with everything."

Salome said, "Maybe so. It must be nice, if that's the case. Or maybe she's just the kind of person who doesn't like to be humiliated, and she felt like Gerald had set her up to look bad in a public place. I mean, apparently it was at this nice restaurant. Joan's friend saw the whole thing and told her about it and then she filled me in."

The bell rang, indicating that a customer was coming in. Salome called out a quick greeting and carefully divested herself of the cat. She said in a hushed voice to me, "Thanks for listening to me, Beatrice."

"I'll pass your message along to Wyatt. And tell Posy I said goodbye. Noo-noo and I are going to head back home."

Soon, Beatrice and Noo-noo were back at home. Beatrice greeted Wyatt who was eating an apple in the living room.

"I have some news," he said with a smile.

"Do we have a new contractor?" asked Beatrice as she lay her keys on the dining room table.

Wyatt said with a smile, "I think we may have. Len meets all the main requirements."

"Which are?"

Wyatt said wryly, "He can start right away, and he's renovated kitchens before."

"Excellent!" said Beatrice.

"I spoke to him on the phone, and he said he'd come by the house soon. How did it go with Noo-noo at Posy's?" Wyatt reached down to pat the little dog, who grinned a doggy grin before lying completely still beside him and falling right to sleep.

"She was a tremendous hit, apparently. Everyone came over to see her, which has made her completely exhausted. She made a new friend with Maisie the cat, too."

"Good," said Wyatt. "Maybe she can go back and visit there a few times while it's noisy here."

There was a jaunty knock at the door, and Beatrice gave Wyatt a weary sigh. "I bet I know who's at the door."

"I won't take that bet because I know who's at the door, too." Wyatt stood up and looked apologetically at her. "I hope it won't seem rude, but I'm going to the back to lie down for a few minutes."

"I totally understand. You've had a long and stressful day, and it's only early afternoon. Maybe you can get a little sleep." Beatrice walked to the front door and peeped out to see Meadow there, as expected. Noo-noo lifted her head to acknowledge the visitor, before laying it back down again and falling right back to sleep.

Meadow practically exploded into the house, full of pent-up energy. "How did the appointment go?" she first asked. "I know Piper said everything was fine, but was it really fine?"

"Perfect. The baby is healthy, Piper is healthy. All is well," said Beatrice quickly, knowing that a drawn-out response would only make Meadow more anxious.

Meadow beamed. "Perfect, indeed. The very answer I was looking for. And now—the murder. I couldn't believe it when Ramsay told me. And, like usual, he didn't give me a single detail! I had to come and pester you on your busy day to find out more."

Beatrice said, "Now Meadow, you know that Ramsay *does* give details to us. He's been very helpful in the past."

"Only when he has the time. And today he's simply not making it. He's only making excuses and spending time with the forensics guys and the state police. It's very vexing," said Meadow, heaving a gusty sigh. "Now tell me what you know." She glanced around the cottage. "Where is poor Wyatt?"

"Wyatt decided to lie down for a little while. I think discovering Gerald this morning took it out of him today," said Beatrice.

Meadow abruptly shifted to a stage whisper, which was practically as loud as her conversational voice before. "The poor man! It must have been an awful shock. But what on earth was he doing there at the factory so early in the morning?" Her tone suggested that Wyatt's predilection for early visits to businesses might have created the problem to begin with.

"Oh, it was a meeting . . . the church HVAC construction. Gerald was supposed to be giving Wyatt the lowest bids for the work. Then Wyatt discovered him."

Meadow said, "And Ramsay said that it was *definitely murder*. No question about it. I thought it more likely that perhaps he was felled by a heart attack, considering the number of hours the man worked. He was quite the workaholic. But Ramsay was quite sure about the fact that it was homicide."

This came as no surprise to Beatrice, since Wyatt had found Gerald tied up to his chair. But she had the feeling that Ramsay didn't want that bit of information divulged to Meadow.

"Horrible!" said Meadow with a snarl. "For such a thing to take place in Dappled Hills! Surely it must be someone from one of the cities, passing through."

Meadow was always fond of the itinerate murderer theory. As if someone from Charlotte or another city had decided to specifically travel to Dappled Hills for the express purpose of killing a resident.

"Don't the police find that the perpetrator is usually someone close to the victim?" asked Beatrice. "Not a random stranger."

"What . . . like Mark Carpenter? Gerald's son? Fiddlesticks! He always seems like a really good person," said Meadow.

Beatrice said thoughtfully, "I don't really know him very well; I've only seen him now and again in church. Would you describe him as friendly? Easy to know?"

Meadow opened her mouth to enthusiastically agree, but then wavered. "Well, I don't know about *very* friendly. I'm sure he'd want to be, but maybe he doesn't really know how. He's the sort of person who's a little socially awkward. But he's supposed to be very, very good at business."

"Yes, he seemed very invested in the family business." Beatrice said, "Oh, never mind me. I'm probably reading too much into it. He just had a huge shock, and people act oddly when they're surprised."

Meadow said, "Did you speak to anybody else? Or, did Mark have any idea who might be behind his father's death? I simply can't imagine it."

Beatrice said, "He did mention Salome Hewitt."

Meadow's mouth became a wide O. "No. It simply isn't possible. She seems like the sweetest thing, and she's a *quilter*."

Beatrice knew better than to try to convince Meadow that quilters could be anything but upright, God-fearing citizens. "It doesn't mean anything . . . she might not have been involved at all. But she definitely has reason to dislike Gerald, it seems." She pressed her lips shut. There was no way that she was going to give away Salome's secret: that her daughter was Gerald's.

Meadow was laser-focused as usual, though. "Why on earth would Salome dislike Gerald? Oh, I suppose you mean because he fired her so abruptly after so many years of loyal service? Yes, that made me very angry with Gerald, myself. Poor Salome was out there trying to fend for herself—and her with a young daughter. The very idea! But, like Salome, *I* can be angry with Gerald and not kill him. It's just that he did an extremely tacky thing."

"That's one word for it," agreed Beatrice.

"It's just fortunate that Salome has folks looking out for her. A sister to take her in. And Posy, who was happy to offer her a job, even though Salome isn't making the money she was before." Meadow made a face. "No, it can't be Salome. Think of someone else."

Beatrice said, "I also spoke to Salome today when I was picking Noo-noo up from the store. Salome did mention that Gerald was having an affair. At least, that's what she believed," she appended quickly as Meadow's eyes and mouth grew large again.

Meadow said, "An *affair*? Who on earth has an affair when he's married to someone like Laura? She's at least ten years younger than he is and looks like a movie star. He was lucky to be married to her, at his age and with his disposition. He had an *affair*?" Meadow's demeanor suggested that Gerald had some nerve.

Beatrice said quickly, "It was someone I didn't know. You likely wouldn't know her."

This seemed to make Meadow feel rather insulted. Meadow considered herself a sort of acting goodwill ambassador for Dappled Hills. A one-woman welcoming committee who'd lived her entire life in the town and wanted nothing more than to make everyone love it as much as she did.

"How could I not know her? How could she know someone like Gerald Carpenter and not me?" demanded Meadow.

Beatrice said in a soothing voice, "Because she doesn't live here. Or, at least, she's not in Dappled Hills most of the time. She has a house in Lenoir."

"But how did Gerald know her? He's not the kind of guy who got out a whole lot. In fact, I think he spent most of his time at the office."

"He did, according to Joan. But apparently not *all* of his time at the office," said Beatrice.

"How on earth did he have the time for an affair?" demanded Meadow.

"From what I understand, he might have been having more than one," said Beatrice with a sigh.

Meadow said, "Wow. I really misjudged him. Here I was thinking he was Mr. Responsibility for putting in so many hours at work and at the church and all the time he was messing around behind everyone's back."

Beatrice said sternly, "This information is obviously between you and me, Meadow. We can't let it go any further. Nobody else knows."

"My lips are sealed," said Meadow

Beatrice said cautiously, "Salome seemed pretty certain. Although, I don't think that information is for public consumption. Besides, Salome said that Gerald called it all off."

"Well, I should think so! He came to his senses, I suppose," said Meadow.

"The woman he was seeing wasn't very happy about it. Apparently, Gerald dumped her in a public place, thinking that she wouldn't make a scene. But she wasn't the kind of woman who appreciated being made a fool of in public, so that approach backfired," said Beatrice.

"Who was this mysterious woman?" asked Meadow with a frown.

"Her name is Colleen Roberts," said Beatrice. "As I said, I didn't know her."

Meadow snorted. "You *should*. In fact, I think you *will*. Very soon. She's a socialite in Lenoir. And I *do* know her. She and I have a couple of mutual friends."

"Well, no wonder I don't know her. I don't exactly hang out with socialites. And I'm not often in Lenoir."

"No, but her daughter is getting married and it's supposed to be this tremendous event. My understanding is that Wyatt is to marry them," said Meadow with a smile.

"Somehow I'm always the last to know these things," said Beatrice, shaking her head. "I don't know if I'm just not paying attention, or if I'm not speaking to the right people."

"It's probably just another wedding to Wyatt," said Meadow with a chuckle. "After all, he performs a zillion of them. But it's actually supposed to be a big deal. Apparently, Colleen chose our church specifically for its 'rustic charm.'" She glanced at her watch. "Okay, I should scoot along. I'll catch up with you later."

Chapter Six

Aﬅer she left, Wyatt poked his head out from the back and looked inquiringly at Beatrice.

"All clear," she said with a chuckle.

He walked sheepishly into the living room and sat down. "Sorry. I just suddenly felt a real lack of energy right when she knocked on the door."

"Oh, I totally understand that. Meadow can sometimes pull the energy right out of a person," said Beatrice. "Were you able to nap?"

"I think I might have driﬅed off for a minute or two, but then my phone rang. It was Edgenora calling from the church office and scheduling a meeting with a mother-of-the-bride," he said.

Beatrice liﬅed her eyebrows. "Was it, by any chance, Colleen Roberts?"

Wyatt blinked at her. "Now how on earth would you know that?"

"Just a lucky guess. Meadow mentioned that her daughter was having a big wedding and that Colleen was very involved in the process."

Wyatt looked puzzled. "I somehow don't even remember that we *know* Colleen."

"I don't think that we do. But her name has come up today as someone who might have known Gerald Carpenter pretty well," said Beatrice.

Wyatt sat down next to her on the sofa and absently patted Noo-noo, who was still taking a nice nap. "You mean that they were involved somehow?"

"That's what I've heard, although I can't confirm it. But it's possible." Beatrice snapped her fingers. "While I'm thinking of it, I was supposed to ask you to schedule a pastoral visit with Salome Hewitt."

Wyatt pulled out his phone and looked at his calendar. "Of course I will. Is she doing all right?" he asked with concern.

"I don't think she is, no. Gerald had apparently fired her recently, and she's been struggling to provide for her daughter." Beatrice paused. "I have the feeling that Salome would rather me prepare you for what the meeting might be dealing with—she feels incredibly guilty that she had an affair with Gerald. An affair that resulted in the birth of her daughter."

Wyatt nodded slowly. "I see. It does sound like she's had a tough time of it lately."

"And we didn't get the full picture of it from Mark this morning."

Wyatt said, "But Mark might not have known. As far as he was concerned, Salome was asking for a raise, and his father was being stingy. It could be that that's as much information as Gerald shared with him. After all, it doesn't exactly put Gerald in a good light. I wouldn't think he'd want to share that information with his son."

There was a tap at the door, and Wyatt and Beatrice stared at each other.

"Well, she *was* gone," said Beatrice, getting up off the sofa. "You can scoot off again, if you want to."

"No, I'm good this time," said Wyatt.

But it wasn't Meadow at all. Instead, a middle-aged woman with blonde hair, red lipstick, and expensive clothing stood outside the door.

"Can I help you?" asked Beatrice.

The woman smiled at her, showing off a perfect set of gleaming teeth. "I'm imposing on you, actually. My name is Colleen Roberts, and my daughter's wedding is coming up in a couple of months. I called the church office, and we set up an appointment with your husband, but I was in the area and thought I'd just run by and see if I could knock this one thing off my list right now. I swear it will only take a few minutes. You have no idea what my list looks like."

Beatrice stood back a bit from the door to let her in, and the woman sailed in, notebook in hand. Wyatt stood up to greet her, and she flashed that perfect smile again.

"How did you know where we lived?" asked Beatrice. She realized that her voice sounded a little tight, but she couldn't really help herself. It was hard enough finding a line between Wyatt's ministry and private life. It didn't help when they were approached at home.

"Oh, Meadow Downey told me. I met her out a few minutes ago, running another errand. She asked me all about Elena's upcoming wedding. You know how Meadow is—she absolutely loves a wedding. And she told me all about your upcoming grandbaby," added Colleen with a rather insincere smile. "Congratulations to you both!"

Beatrice had no doubt that Meadow had told her. And probably a lot more than Colleen wished to hear.

"Thank you," said Wyatt politely. "Please, won't you sit down?"

It was a fairly rhetorical question since Colleen was already on her way to one of their floral, overstuffed armchairs.

"A coffee maybe?" asked Beatrice dryly.

"Would you? I'm a little on the sleepy side today, I have to admit." Colleen glanced over at the kitchen and made a face. "Wow. Looks like you're having some work done."

Wyatt said, "A bit of kitchen renovation, although the work has stalled out recently. We're hoping it will be knocked out soon with a new contractor. But the coffee maker is right here in the living room now, so no worries." He poured her a coffee, adding cream and sugar at Colleen's request.

"Anyway, Meadow told me that you were both home when I asked her," said Colleen carelessly. "I just couldn't help myself."

Nor, guessed Beatrice, had she wanted to.

Wyatt handed her the coffee. "What is it that we can help you with?"

Colleen opened her notebook and said, "The wedding preparations, of course. But not just that. I heard from Meadow that you both had a very disturbing morning."

Wyatt grew solemn. "It was."

Colleen gave him a considering look. "I'm actually a friend of Gerald's. I was terribly shocked to hear about his death. And Meadow seemed to think that it wasn't an accident at all? That he was murdered?"

Beatrice said, "The police are definitely investigating his death."

Colleen blew out a breath. "That is just so hard to believe. Why, I only saw Gerald recently. There I was, having a quiet morning at home in Lenoir, and all the while poor Gerald was lying dead in his office. What a horrible thing."

"I'm sorry for your loss," said Wyatt kindly. "You said that you and Gerald were friends?"

Colleen opened her mouth as if to say something and then apparently had second thoughts and revised it. "We were. Like I say, I can't believe it." She paused. "Although I know Gerald and his daughter didn't get along all that well." Her eyes grew wide. "You don't think that *Joan* could have anything to do with his death? I mean, they really *didn't* get along. Gerald was always complaining about her. He said that she was always asking him for money for one thing or another."

Wyatt said, "We don't know anything else about it, I'm afraid. I'm sorry, I've got some business I need to attend to later. Was there something regarding the wedding plans that you wanted to go over?"

Beatrice hid a smile. Wyatt was able to finesse everything in a non-offensive way.

Colleen gave a simpering smile. "Yes. Dear Elena's wedding. I want everything to be perfect!"

The only problem was that Colleen's idea of perfect and the rules that the church had established for weddings were not aligned. Colleen wanted candles everywhere (and there was a maximum for those, per the fire code). Colleen wanted to attach bows to the pew ends with tacks. Colleen wanted aisle runners in the sanctuary, which were safety hazards for both young and old. Colleen wanted the flower girls to drop real flower petals—which would stain the carpet —instead of silk ones.

Wyatt listened very carefully to everything that Colleen said. Then he said, "I can promise you that your daughter will have a beautiful wedding at our church."

Beatrice added quickly, "All of the brides talk about the natural setting and the church's history as adding so much to the ceremony."

Colleen kept quiet, but her face was a little pinched as if she expected to hear some bad news coming her way regarding her careful plans.

"Unfortunately, church policy dictates that some of the added decorations you want for the service aren't going to be possible," said Wyatt in a polite, but firm voice.

This clearly didn't sit very well with Colleen. "I'm sure that we can come to some sort of agreement," she said smoothly. "Perhaps a sizable donation to one of the church's favorite charities?"

Wyatt said, "That's very generous of you, but it isn't possible for the church to make exceptions for a single wedding."

Colleen narrowed her eyes and seemed about to argue the point further. Instead, she bared her teeth at them in a smile and said, "I see. Well, we can talk more about this at a future date.

I can promise you, this wedding will be very helpful for your church in terms of publicity. I'm inviting all kinds of really fabulous people, and I know quite a few celebrities that are planning on attending. You'll end up with great press and photographs. Anyway, as I said, we'll talk about this again soon. Good to meet both of you."

Once Colleen had left and Wyatt had politely closed the door behind her, he leaned back against it and gave Beatrice a look.

"I know," she said with a chuckle. "That must have been completely exhausting for you."

"Every single thing that she wanted to do was against church policy," he said in wonder. "Every single thing. That must be a record."

"You said the magic words, though: *church policy*. It's not Wyatt Thompson's policy. The church deacons and elders came up with these rules, and for good reason. Otherwise, the church would have either a fire on its hands or expensive cleanups," said Beatrice.

"So you do think she was being unreasonable?" said Wyatt.

"Most definitely. But you were able to stand your ground *and* appear sympathetic at the same time. I don't know how you did it."

Wyatt walked over to drop onto the sofa. "Well, at least we won't have to worry about that wedding now. I think we got it all straightened out between us in terms of expectations."

Beatrice said, "I hate to say this, but she's exactly the person you *should* worry about. She's the kind of person who smiles and nods when you're carefully explaining the rules and then goes off and does exactly what she wants to."

Wyatt frowned. "You think she might show up on her daughter's wedding day with candles, real flowers, and aisle runners?"

"I absolutely do. And then I'd expect her to blink and look completely innocent and say that it wasn't explained to her," said Beatrice.

"But I did send her out with a wedding guidelines document," said Wyatt slowly.

"I'd follow back up soon with a digital version and tell her that there was a new church policy in place that families must sign the guidelines and send them back in. Then keep the document on record in case there's any trouble," said Beatrice.

Wyatt said, "That's an excellent idea. I'll follow up with her soon."

Beatrice said, "What did you think about everything else that she said?"

Wyatt said, "She certainly seemed curious about Gerald's death. And eager to implicate his daughter."

"I think there's a lot more to her friendship with Gerald than she let on. That's what Salome was saying, too." Beatrice stopped talking as there was a rap at the door. Noo-noo perked her ears up and trotted to the door. "Maybe that's Len, here to save us from a destroyed kitchen."

"Let's hope," said Wyatt heavily.

Wyatt opened the door to see a large, bearded man in overalls. The man bobbed his head in greeting and said, "Thanks for taking me on." He reached down and scratched Noo-noo behind her ears.

Wyatt said, "Good to meet you, Len. Let me show you the project and we can talk about costs and how much time it might take."

Len nodded and said, "If we can come to an agreement, I can start this afternoon because the materials I needed for another job haven't arrived yet."

Wyatt glanced over at Beatrice, and she smiled. "I'll take Noo-noo back over to the Patchwork Cottage. And this time I think I may take something to work on with me."

A few minutes later, Beatrice was driving a grinning Noo-noo back over to the Patchwork Cottage.

Posy greeted her as soon as she came in through the door. "Beatrice! I'm glad that you came back. Does this mean that you're actually getting some work done at home?"

Beatrice said, "We are. At least, it looks like we are, as long as Wyatt and Len agree on the terms of the work. At any rate, I think Noo-noo and I need a break from it all! Since everything went so well this morning, I figured that she and I could maybe spend a little time here? I know I need to get some quilting done."

"Of course you can! And Maisie will be happy to have you here, too."

Sure enough, as if on cue, Maisie the shop cat came trotting over to Noo-noo and bumped her head against Noo-noo's.

Posy said, "It's pretty quiet at the shop now, so you should be able to make some progress. Is this one of your projects for Piper?"

Beatrice sat down on the sofa in the shop's sitting area. "I'm afraid so," she said wryly. "Although I'm definitely under a deadline at this point, obviously. It's a diaper bag, and it's been a little trickier than I thought it would be. I've finished with the burp cloths, thankfully. And Meadow has made a slew of bibs and other things."

Beatrice pulled the diaper bag out of the tote she was carrying and showed it to Posy.

"You've done a great job so far, even if you did think it was tricky. Have you gotten stuck with it or have you just run out of time?" asked Posy.

"Oh, it's definitely a time issue, for sure. I did run into a couple of places where I wasn't sure how to move forward with it, but Meadow gave me a few tips. At this point, I think it's just a race against the clock," said Beatrice.

The bell on the door rang, and Posy walked toward the door to greet the customer. She paused as she saw that it was Joan Carpenter, Gerald's daughter, looking pale and stressed.

Chapter Seven

Posy didn't hesitate at all, but quickly gave her a wordless hug. Joan gave her a tight squeeze back and then pulled away to swab her face with a tissue that she was already holding in her hand for such an eventuality.

Beatrice didn't know Joan quite as well. Joan was a quilter in another guild, the Cut-Ups and had spotty attendance at church, where Beatrice would only have the chance to speak briefly with her. Posy knew her as a customer at the shop.

Posy said to Joan, "I'm just so sorry. Of course I heard the bad news this morning."

Joan said, "Thanks. Dad was always such a huge presence in my life that it's hard to believe he's gone." She paused. "I don't think I can stand to be at home any longer, so I decided to come here and spend a little time. I was hoping to talk to Salome while I was here, too."

"Oh, I'm sorry. Salome has gone home for the day. Can I call her for you to see if she might be able to come back?" asked Posy.

Joan gave a quick shake of her head. "No, no. She'll be spending time with that sweet daughter of hers, and I don't want to intrude on that. Will she be here tomorrow?"

"She sure will . From nine to two tomorrow, I think."

Joan said, "I'll try to catch up with her then. Is it all right if I sit here and quilt and chat for a bit? I think it will help me to calm down some. I brought one of my projects, just in case."

"Absolutely! And you might know Beatrice Thompson? She's here quilting and brought her corgi, Noo-noo. She's very cuddly," said Posy in a persuasive tone.

Noo-noo grinned at Joan and wagged her nubbin of a tail.

Joan smiled. "I think I could use a cuddly corgi right about now. You've convinced me. And I do know Beatrice." She turned around to face the sitting area and raised her hand in greeting before heading in Beatrice's direction. The bell on the door rang again, and Posy was off to help a new quilter find supplies for her home.

Beatrice stood up in greeting as Joan approached. Joan quickly said, "Oh, please sit down, Beatrice. You're in the middle of a project, I see." She looked closer at what Beatrice was working on and said, "For Piper? It's adorable. I love that you have Piper's monogram on there and the multi-colored owls are precious. Piper must be so excited. Isn't it getting very close to time for the baby to arrive?"

Beatrice sat back down and watched as Noo-noo plopped down on top of Joan's feet as Joan sat across from Beatrice. Joan ran her hand through the soft fur around Noo-noo's neck and seemed to relax a little.

"She is and Meadow and I are practically apoplectic, we're so thrilled," said Beatrice dryly. "I'm not sure how much Piper is going to even be able to hold her own baby in the first few days."

She paused and said, "Joan, I'm so terribly sorry about your father. It must have been such an awful shock."

Joan's face was hidden by her hair as she bent over to stroke Noo-noo around her ears. Then a few seconds later, she raised her head and said, "It was, it really was. But Mark said that he felt so much better with Wyatt there and that Wyatt had found Dad. It must have been a terrible morning for him, though."

Beatrice nodded. "But he was glad to be there to help, however he could. He thought a lot of Gerald and Gerald was a big part of the church."

Joan said, "Like I was telling Posy, I just never believed that anything could happen to Dad. He was always *stalwart*. So strong, so strong-minded. He seemed completely indestructible to me." She took a deep breath. "I'm sorry," she added, her voice breaking.

"Oh goodness, don't apologize! Of course you're going to be upset. We can talk about other things." She gave a rueful laugh. "I could talk about upcoming baby preparations until you're ready to run away, believe me. Or there's always my horrific tale of kitchen renovation, if we're really desperate."

She was pleased to see a small smile on Joan's face. "Thanks, Beatrice. Honestly, I think it will help me to sort it all out in my head if I talk it over. Is that all right?"

"Absolutely. Or you know that Wyatt would love to speak with you, too." Wyatt was trained to handle all of these tough conversations that Beatrice seemed to be having today.

But Joan shook her head. "Nope. Minister's wife is close enough. Besides, we'll be keeping Wyatt busy enough with the funeral plans. I think my problem with Dad's death is guilt."

Beatrice said, "Guilt is a hard one to handle, for sure."

Joan looked relieved at this affirmation and quickly continued, "It's true. And I'll be honest . . . I haven't historically had the best relationship with Dad. He's always been so interested in the family business. I know he wanted *me* to be interested in it, but I just wasn't. I couldn't summon the enthusiasm that he thought I should have. I mean, I was proud of him for developing such a well-known and respected business. Of course I was. But it wasn't what I wanted to spend my life doing."

Beatrice was having a tough time remembering exactly what it was that Joan did.

Fortunately, Joan filled her in. "I'm a nurse. So being in the pimento cheese business wasn't exactly what I wanted to choose to fulfill me, as you can imagine. Although I think the pimento cheese is very tasty!" The last was tacked on with a roll of her eyes.

"I'm sure your father didn't want to force you into the family business," said Beatrice. "Do you just feel badly about it because you know it's what he wanted?"

"He was *so* disappointed. But I didn't want my whole life to be sucked in by that company the way he was. Mark is different—he's business-minded anyway and enjoyed being in an office, doing paperwork, and managing people. He's much more like Dad. But I didn't have warm fuzzy feelings for the family business. It took Dad away for my entire childhood. He was never there at the school play or field day or parent night at school." Joan made a face.

"I'm so sorry," said Beatrice. "That must have been very tough not having him around."

"It was. I mean, my mother tried. But there was only so much that she could really keep up with at one time. She didn't have any help with the house then. And she was trying to get us to our activities and cook meals and do laundry. She was run ragged." Her lips tightened. "I know you're relatively new to town and might not know how Mom died. Mark and I were teenagers. Mom was actually running an errand the night she died. She'd finally asked Dad to do *one thing*. And that was because I pleaded with her to give him *something*. She asked him to pick up a carton of milk on his way home from work."

Beatrice winced. "And he forgot?"

"He did. Or simply didn't care at all. He wasn't the one who drank it or who put it in his cereal in the morning. By then, the weather had gotten pretty bad outside, and Mom was never a wonderful driver. Anyway, she lost control on the mountain roads." Joan's voice broke again, and she paused for a few moments. "I'm sorry. It's been such a long time that you'd think I'd be over it by now."

Beatrice leaned forward and squeezed her hand. "But you've had the kind of upsetting day that would bring it all back to anyone."

Joan smiled at her. "You're right. Anyway, things have been weird at home since then. Dad still spent a ton of time at the office, so Mark and I basically raised ourselves. He did finally think about getting a housekeeper to help out at the house, and Mark and I took turns cooking some basic meals. We got by." She sighed. "And then Dad met Laura."

Beatrice said, "I don't really know her very well, I'm afraid."

"Who does? She's always been something of a mystery to me. I don't think Laura is at all shaken up by my father's death. They had very separate lives in many ways. She was always happy to go to events with him and be the eye candy on his arm, but the day-to-day life here in Dappled Hills didn't seem to interest her very much. She never really made any friends here." She paused again. "I think she was only with Dad because he gave her a very comfortable life. I wouldn't be at all surprised if she marries again, and quickly."

Beatrice watched as Maisie walked over to curl up against Noo-noo. Noo-noo opened one eye and then shut it again. She felt as if Joan needed to talk herself out—she was happy to just be a sounding board and listen for a while.

But Joan quickly said, "Hey, I'm sorry, Beatrice. Here you are trying to relax for a while and work on your grandbaby's diaper bag and I'm dumping all my troubles on you."

"You're not doing anything of the sort, Joan. I'm happy to listen to you—I can only imagine that your head must be spinning after the day you've had. If it helps you at all to tell me some of what's going on, I'm very happy to be an ear. And I've worked myself up to the place where I can quilt as well as listen." She laughed. "Although it did take a little while. Meadow could tell you stories about some of my first quilts."

Joan said, "Thanks, Beatrice. You don't know how much I appreciate it. And you're absolutely right about my head spinning. I think I need to talk it all out. I don't really have anything *against* Laura. It's just that I don't think she's ever really cared to be a big part of this family. Plus, there was some extra tension because of the potential sale of the business."

Beatrice glanced up from the diaper bag to look at Joan with surprise. "I didn't realize that the business was going to be sold."

Joan said, "It wasn't a done deal, by any means. And, if you'd asked Dad, he'd have said that the business would be sold over his dead body." She stopped and put her hand over her mouth, her eyes wide. Then she gave a nervous laugh. "What an awful thing to say. What I meant to say is that Dad would never have willingly sold his business. It was like his baby. He built it from nothing into a really successful company, and it was never his intention to ever sell it."

Beatrice said slowly, "But other people thought it might be a good idea to sell the business?"

"Yes. Mark was one of them. There was a reputable firm that was interested in buying the company, and he wasn't sure that we'd get another great offer. He thought it was a good time to sell. Laura agreed with him," said Joan.

"And you?" asked Beatrice gently.

Joan threw up her hands. "I never really liked the business to begin with, considering all the time my father spent working. I figured if Mark thought it was a good time to sell, then maybe we should consider it. He was the business major, after all."

Beatrice said, "Did everyone share their thoughts with your father?"

Joan snorted. "That's phrasing it nicely. Mark was rather pushy, which I knew was going to be a bad approach with Dad. If you push anything at Dad, he's going to push right back, no matter what it is. Laura did her passive-aggressive thing with Dad about the sale, and he absolutely hated that. And I suppose

I probably whined about it." She sighed. "We sound like quite a group. No wonder Dad wasn't very receptive."

"He did consider it, though?" asked Beatrice.

"Only on the surface. Mark had already set up one or two meetings and asked if Dad would at least hear them out. And they were important men from important companies, so he did. But he didn't really *listen*. I guess now that Dad is gone, Mark will be free to do what he likes with the company."

Beatrice nodded, but looked troubled.

"I suppose that gives him a motive," added Joan slowly. "But Mark wouldn't hurt a fly. Violence wouldn't fit into his business plan. And, believe me, Mark is a planner." She glanced at her watch. "Speaking of planning, I should get out of here. We're supposed to meet up with Laura and make some preliminary plans for the funeral service before we meet with Wyatt later. Thanks so much for lending an ear, Beatrice."

She gave Beatrice a warm smile, gave Noo-noo another absent rub, and left.

Beatrice quietly hand-stitched for a few minutes while Posy helped the customer to check out her materials. Then Posy came over to join her.

"Everything all right with Joan?" she asked with concern. "I feel so bad for her."

Beatrice said, "I think so, although I know she's shocked about her father's death. She said he just seemed so impervious to everything." She kept Joan's feelings of guilt to herself since she knew Joan was speaking to her in private.

The bell on the door rang again, and they glanced up. It was Edgenora, one of the Village Quilters and the administrative assistant for Wyatt at the church. Beatrice glanced at her watch, having the feeling that it was later in the day than she'd realized. Sure enough, the church office would have closed for the day ten minutes ago, and Posy would be closing in about an hour. Edgenora waved and joined them. "Thought I'd run by here and pick up some more fabric. I've been so distracted lately that somehow I miscalculated the amount I needed and then ran out right in the middle of piecing the quilt top."

Posy wrinkled her brow. "You're working on the Album Cross pattern, right?"

Edgenora said, "That's right. I don't know how you always remember. I hope you have some more left—I didn't even consider that you might have run out."

Posy said quickly, "Don't you worry, I have plenty of it."

They walked over to a display that had the fabric, and Posy measured it out. After Edgenora made her purchase, she walked back over to see Beatrice.

"I'm almost scared to ask how the kitchen renovation is going," she said with a wince. "Wyatt seemed so worried about it when I talked to him about it earlier."

Beatrice smiled at her. She was a huge fan of Edgenora's because she did a fantastic job as a church secretary. Before Edgenora came on board, Beatrice had found herself fielding a lot of church-related phone calls: everything from questions about whether the church league soccer game would be cancelled for rain to what time the yoga class was. Now Edgenora not only fielded those calls herself, she also kept up with an online church calendar that everyone could refer to. Plus, she'd become a good friend and was always a very rational person to talk to . . . something Beatrice appreciated.

"Fingers crossed, we're in better shape now than we were in yesterday! The project completely stalled out because Dale had to stop work, but his cousin is on the job now and is supposed to be working at this moment. Noo-noo isn't crazy about the loud noises of construction, so we're here giving her a break," said Beatrice.

Edgenora said, "Well, that's good news! I know you're tired of eating sandwiches and yogurts."

Edgenora asked how Piper was doing. They chatted for a few minutes and then Edgenora said, "I actually wanted to ask you about this morning. I heard about Gerald Carpenter."

"Isn't it awful?" asked Beatrice.

"Yes, what an awful morning. Gerald was a good man and was certainly organized. Whenever he'd call the church office to update us on bids for the HVAC work, he never wasted a second, but gave us all the information clearly and succinctly. I went with Wyatt for one meeting with Gerald over in Gerald's office. He had the most amazingly-organized file system I think I've ever seen." There was a wistful note in Edgenora's voice. If there was one thing she appreciated, it was good organization. "Unfortunately, we don't have his latest report on the bids, but it can definitely wait."

"Did you have any impressions of Gerald at all, personally?" Beatrice asked. "I feel as if I didn't really know him very well."

Edgenora said, "You and I are both new to town compared to most people. I don't think Gerald was one of those people that one got to know unless they've been here most of their lives. He seemed private to me."

Or secretive, Beatrice thought.

Edgenora continued, "And I suppose was a bit gruff with his staff. He definitely had a no-nonsense air about him. He was not the sort of person who joked around with employees or who was a company favorite. No, he seemed like he was all business all the time. Although that's probably how he became so successful. He was driven."

"Do you know his family well?" asked Beatrice.

"No. His son, to a certain degree. Gerald acted rather gruff around *him*, too, as I recall. Mark came into his office while we were there, and Gerald snapped his head off. Then he snapped his assistant's head off later, too. He'd apparently directed her that he was not to be disturbed while he was in a meeting with us, and she'd thought his son might be excluded from that directive. But he wasn't."

Beatrice nodded and said apologetically, "I know I'm asking a lot of questions today."

Edgenora gave her a smile. "You are, but why wouldn't you be? You had a very confusing morning and you're trying to work it all out in your head."

"This next question may seem unrelated. I was just wondering if you knew or had any impressions of a woman who is planning on having a wedding at our church. Or, rather, planning her *daughter's* wedding."

Edgenora pursed her lips. "You must be speaking of Colleen Roberts."

Chapter Eight

Beatrice laughed. "And you know everyone, short time in town or not."

"Colleen is one of those I'd know, no matter what, I'm afraid." Edgenora kept her voice low. "She seems like trouble to me, Beatrice. She is so pushy and she wants everything done her way. The times that she's called into the church, she didn't even want to leave messages—she wanted to be connected to Wyatt right away."

Beatrice nodded. "I thought the same thing. Listening to her talk to Wyatt about plans, I wondered if her daughter cared about or even knew all the plans that her mother had for her wedding."

"Exactly. She seemed like the kind of mother-of-the-bride who just takes the planning over completely. Actually, she seems like the kind of person who'd do that even if there *wasn't* a wedding—she's simply not good at group work," said Edgenora. "I was just concerned from her entitled attitude that she was going to make some unreasonable demands of the church."

"She already has," said Beatrice wryly. "But don't worry—Wyatt shot down all of her ideas in his very gentle way."

Edgenora knit her brow. "Although she might say one thing and do another."

Beatrice smiled. "You have a very astute reading of people. I thought exactly the same thing. I told Wyatt that it would be a good idea if he drew up a contract and said that it was a new required document for the church. That might make things more official . . . laying out exactly what the rules are."

Edgenora took out a notepad from her voluminous purse. "An excellent suggestion. And I know a way to make it even more official—we have an attorney who's also a member. He asked me recently if we'd like him to look over wording for permission forms for youth activities and so forth. I bet he wouldn't mind if we asked him to glance over the form."

"That would be *perfect*," said Beatrice, beaming at her. "You're a jewel." She paused for a second and then said, "I know you hear a lot as a church admin assistant. Have you heard anything else regarding Colleen? Has anyone mentioned if she's in a relationship of any kind?"

Edgenora lifted a brow. "I only know what Colleen herself demonstrated in the parking lot of the church. I was on my way home at the end of the day and saw her jogging up to a man and laying quite a kiss on him. I pretended that I didn't see and hurried on my way," she added with a sniff.

"And the man?" Beatrice asked, holding her breath.

Edgenora said slowly, "Well, ordinarily I wouldn't want to mention it, but considering it's you, Beatrice, I will. It was Gerald Carpenter."

Beatrice nodded. "Thank you. I was just trying to confirm something that I'd heard. I knew that if anybody knew, it would probably be you."

Edgenora said, "It was certainly the wrong place and the wrong time for such a display. And I have to say that Gerald Carpenter looked quite put out about it. He was very stern and jerked away from her quickly. He even looked as if he was brushing himself off after the contact with Colleen."

Beatrice frowned. "So Colleen was already planning the ceremony before getting in touch with Wyatt?"

Edgenora gave her a wry look. "That's correct. She was scouting out locations just like someone in the film industry. She called me twice about it. The first time, she called to let me know that she wanted to walk around the church campus. But it started raining, so she was only able to see the interior buildings that day. She had me unlock everything and took pictures and notes of the bride's dressing room and the sanctuary. Then she called another time to say that she was going to be walking around outside the church, once the weather was good. It might have been that day that she saw Gerald in the parking lot."

"What was Colleen's reaction when Gerald pulled away from her?" asked Beatrice curiously.

Edgenora said, "It didn't seem to bother her much because she burst out in these gales of laughter and told him to loosen up." She made a face. "And she *does* seem like the kind of person who's loosened up. I know that she's not very particular about paying her bills on time. We have a deposit for reserving the church for a wedding, and it has gone unpaid. And it's an *important* fee. We'll have to run the air conditioning and the lights during the ceremony, engage the organist to play, and Wyatt will officiate. The custodian will need to clean afterwards. These are expenses that must be addressed."

Beatrice said, "With any luck, she'll send in a check soon. Perhaps it's just slipped her mind with all the other planning she's doing. I know Piper and I have been very absentminded and we're only planning for a baby's arrival, not a whole wedding."

Edgenora glanced at her watch. It was a big watch and one that kept her on track all day long at the church. She'd also purchased for the church office a large clock with big numbers that she put directly in front of her desk. If there was one thing that Edgenora was good at, it was running on time. "I should leave within five minutes, I'm afraid. I'm meeting Savannah for a quick bite to eat and a movie."

Beatrice quickly felt a slight guilty feeling when Edgenora mentioned Savannah. Life had been very busy lately between attending activities at the church and volunteering there and helping Piper get ready for the new baby. Savannah was one of her quilt guild friends that she'd been meaning to catch up with. Although she'd seen her at the baby shower, it wasn't the kind of event where you could really talk with someone for a long period of uninterrupted time. "How is Savannah doing?"

Edgenora gave a fond smile. "She's doing much better! You know how I was fussing that she wasn't eating really well? She's actually added a couple of healthy recipes to her cooking repertoire."

Beatrice smiled. "So she's stepping away from mac and cheese and canned soups?" Savannah's sister, Georgia, had been the cook of the two sisters. But Georgia had married, and Savannah had fallen into bad habits when she was no longer cooking for them.

"Oh, I wouldn't say that she's stepping *away* from them. No. Nor the Pop Tarts. But she's added some easy healthy snacks and meals into her rotation," said Edgenora with a smile.

Edgenora stood up and reached down to give Noo-noo a goodbye pat. "I'll see you soon, Beatrice. Have Wyatt shoot over that form we talked about, and I'll have the lawyer take a look."

"Perfect. Will do," said Beatrice.

Beatrice and Posy visited for a few minutes after Edgenora left and then Beatrice decided that it was time to set off for home. She put Noo-noo back on her leash, and they were on their way.

Len's work truck was gone when she arrived, and Beatrice entered the house with some degree of trepidation. Had anything been done at all?

Walking in, she saw that progress had been made. Wyatt lifted his head and grinned at her. "Well, it's not finished, but Len did manage to get some work done before he left again."

"That's great! At least we're better off and further along than we were this morning." Beatrice took Noo-noo's leash off and the little dog walked around on a sniffing expedition.

"He says he'll be able to come out tomorrow around lunch, too," said Wyatt.

"Fingers crossed that's actually the case," said Beatrice.

"It will give me time to meet with Laura Carpenter, Gerald's widow. She called and arranged for us to meet around ten tomorrow morning to go over arrangements for Gerald's funeral. His children will be there, too," said Wyatt.

Beatrice said thoughtfully, "I probably should run some food by, too."

Wyatt snapped his fingers. "I'm glad you mentioned that. Meadow called and is planning on bringing food, too. She wanted to go over there with you since she didn't know Laura as well as she knew Gerald."

"Maybe we can get there before you come by to meet with the family regarding the arrangements," said Beatrice. "Did Meadow say what she was bringing?" Beatrice knew that whatever it was, it would be good. Meadow was a master of home cooking and everything she made was delicious. Unfortunately, it was now evening, and Beatrice had no kitchen and no ideas of what to bring a grieving widow.

Wyatt said, "She was providing a fried chicken dinner with all the fixings, apparently. But she suggested that you pick up breakfast and then most of the day's food would be provided for."

Beatrice felt relieved. "That's perfect, actually. I wasn't sure how I was going to pull off even making a side dish for the meal with the kitchen the way it is. When I get up tomorrow, I can pick up muffins and doughnuts from June Bug's."

With everything on her mind, Beatrice's sleep was unfortunately spotty. She gave up early in the morning and got up. First, she made a list of all the things that she could think of that she needed to do. That way, her mind wouldn't be spinning with all the uncompleted tasks. Then she picked up her book to do a little reading. She and Wyatt were reading the same book and

Beatrice found that she'd gotten behind while Wyatt had been overseeing the construction in the kitchen while reading. They'd chosen *All the Light We Cannot See*. Beatrice had been looking forward to a return to novel reading after she'd read a nonfiction selection that Wyatt had chosen over the last few books. She really needed to put the finishing touches on that diaper bag, but figured that she could work that in over the next couple of days.

Wyatt joined her in the living room at seven. "Everything all right?" he asked, rubbing his eyes as he adjusted to the light in the room.

"I just couldn't sleep well and didn't want to disturb you. Now that you're up, I think I'll get ready to head over to June Bug's. Want me to pick up some breakfast for us, while I'm there?"

"That would be great. Otherwise, we'll probably be eating more yogurt," said Wyatt with a wry smile.

So Beatrice set off for the bakery while Wyatt took Noonoo for a short walk and then fed her. It was early enough that Beatrice figured June Bug might still be in the process of baking, but when she walked into the shop, the little wide-eyed woman seemed to be already finished.

June Bug gave her a shy smile as Beatrice greeted her. The shop, as always, smelled delicious. She saw that there were already cakes out, too, as well as the morning pastries.

"How is Piper doing?" June Bug asked. Her expression always made her look a little anxious.

"She's doing great! She and the baby both are, according to the doctor visit we had yesterday. Oh, and be sure to thank Katie for me again for her sweet gift for the baby. That stuffed cat is absolutely adorable with her little bow-tie and those big eyes. I know the baby is going to love her."

June Bug smiled shyly at her. "She called her Tilly, but wanted the baby to name her however she wanted. Because Tilly was so special, she wanted her to be loved by another child."

"That's so sweet of her. How is Katie doing? We didn't have time to catch up much at the baby shower," said Beatrice.

June Bug proudly found a piece of paper that was in a small stack behind the counter and showed it to her.

"All As on her report card!" said Beatrice. "You must be so proud. I know you've been working hard with her."

June Bug had told her all about helping Katie with her spelling words and math. When Katie had moved, she'd been a little behind her grade at the new school. Clearly now she'd caught up—and then some.

"She's been working hard, too," said June Bug with a happy twinkle in her eyes. "And now she has new friends and can play just as hard as she works." She nodded to the small office. "She's already getting ahead today on schoolwork. I bring her here with me in the mornings, of course . . . we both have to get up really early. She likes to do her reading now when it's so quiet."

"That's wonderful to hear. Tell her that I said congratulations on the great report card. Although I know you're a great example of hard work—it looks like you've already finished your baking for today," said Beatrice.

June Bug nodded and showed Beatrice what she'd been working on. It wasn't easy for Beatrice to choose. There were buttermilk biscuits, banana bread, quiches, scones, cinnamon buns, and muffins.

"You're making it very hard on me today," said Beatrice with a grin.

June Bug looked pleased.

Since Beatrice couldn't really decide, she asked for two different plates with a variety of breads on them. That way, *June Bug* could choose.

A few minutes later, June Bug carefully put the plates into plastic bags for Beatrice to carry back home and gave her a cheerful goodbye as the bakery phone rang with an order

When Beatrice got back home, she held one of the bags up to show Wyatt. "We have a feast!"

He grinned at her. "That's perfect. I didn't really feel like cereal this morning since I've been eating cereal for supper some nights."

"Well, we have lots to choose from. And I got a plate of goodies for Laura, too, of course. June Bug had so many pastries out that I had a tough time making up my mind."

After they ate and drank some more coffee, Wyatt left to go to the office to get some things done before heading over to the Carpenter house. After he left, there was a loud knock at the door which set Noo-noo to barking excitedly. Beatrice smiled to herself. Meadow had clearly arrived.

Meadow bustled in. "Good morning! I had to see your kitchen disaster for myself. I was so distracted yesterday that it was the last thing on my mind." She peered over and made a face. "You've been living like this for a while. How are the two of you surviving?"

Beatrice laughed. "Pretty well because we've been eating out or bringing food in. This morning we had a variety of baked goods from June Bug's."

Meadow snorted. "Then you've been eating better than we have. I've been so busy with the baby stuff that poor Ramsay acts as though I've been starving him. He's pitiful! Keeps asking when I'll go back to making my famous big breakfasts. He's been eating grocery store bagels for the last couple of weeks because I just don't have it in me to cook in the mornings."

"What have you been doing for the baby?" asked Beatrice curiously.

"Whatever Ash tells me still needs to be done," said Meadow. "Although sometimes he's not the most reliable person to ask, so I've asked Piper."

Beatrice made a face. "And I thought *I* was helping out. I didn't realize there was so much to still be done. The way that Piper has talked about it, I thought they had everything in hand."

Meadow gestured toward her car, and Beatrice grabbed the platter of food and stepped outside. Meadow said, "They do. I think they're having to find things for me to do because otherwise I drive them crazy checking on Piper. They've had me help put a wallpaper border up, make a changing pad for the changing table, hang some open bins for storage on the walls. At this point, they're probably wringing their hands trying to think of other things to keep me busy. It may have gotten to the point where Ash has me doing their yardwork."

They got into the car, and Beatrice said dryly, "I'm sure if you were to ask Wyatt, there are any number of things that you could volunteer for at the church to kill time."

Meadow started up the car. "By golly, you're right. I wasn't thinking about volunteering because it's such a short period of time until the baby comes—and then I really *will* have lots to do. But the church probably has short-term volunteering opportunities?"

Beatrice clutched the platter as Meadow lurched out of the driveway and swung onto the road. "Let's just say that any time you wanted to head over there and babysit in *any* nursery for a service or for a yoga class or any number of nurseries, you wouldn't be turned down."

"Good point," said Meadow thoughtfully. "So I could volunteer in the infant nursery, for instance? I probably could stand to brush up on my baby skills. It's been a long time since I last cared for a baby."

Unfortunately, Meadow was now putting a lot more thought into volunteering in the church nursery than she was in driving the vehicle.

"Look out!" said Beatrice—pointing ahead at an old Lincoln, driving mostly in their lane, careening toward them.

Meadow swerved off the side of the road and came to a stop. They saw Miss Sissy shaking her arthritic fist at them as she drove off.

Meadow said faintly, "Oops." And then, with more certainty, "Miss Sissy is a danger to the roadways. Someone should take her keys away from her."

Beatrice took a deep breath and looked at Meadow through narrowed eyes. Perhaps someone should start thinking about taking the keys away from Meadow.

Meadow put the car in motion again, this time driving a bit more sedately and with more focus.

Fortunately, after the curve was Gerald's house. It was a rambling brick home with ivy scaling the outside walls, and the home was located on top of a steep hill. The yard was carefully maintained with bushes clipped perfectly and a bed of roses on the side of the house.

Meadow said, "They must have some fantastic mountain views from the back."

Beatrice said, "I've never actually been here. And, in fact, Wyatt mentioned earlier that it would be his first visit out to their house."

"Really? I'd have thought he'd have been out here, considering all the church-related work he did with Gerald," said Meadow as they got out of the car and started walking down the driveway to the front door.

Chapter Nine

"Wyatt said that Gerald always wanted to meet at the office," said Beatrice. "And very early. Apparently, Gerald was a man who liked to follow strict routines. He'd get any church-related or personal-related business out of the way first, before he started in on work."

Meadow rang the doorbell, and the door was immediately answered by Laura Carpenter. She was a tall, slender woman in her 50s—a good deal younger than Gerald. Although her eyes were sad, there was a surprising lack of expression in her face. A moment later, Beatrice realized that Laura had likely had some work done—Botox can have the effect of not just minimizing wrinkles, but minimizing emotions, too.

Laura pulled both of them toward her for a hug. "Aren't you both so sweet? I'm lucky to have folks who care about us. I know that Gerald would be very touched." As she said Gerald's name, she pulled out a tissue to dab at her perfectly-made-up eyes.

Meadow said, "Well of course we wanted to come by! We have breakfast and supper for you. And if y'all eat this platter full of June Bug's delicacies, I'm sure you won't have any appetite for lunch at all. So you should be set for the day. Which way is the kitchen and I'll put the chicken away?"

"You're a dear," said Laura. "It's just through the archway there and will be the third door on your left."

Beatrice asked as Meadow obediently trotted off to the kitchen, "Would you like me to leave the platter somewhere more accessible, in case you'd like to snack from it soon?"

Laura beamed at her, white teeth glinting. "That would be lovely. I didn't eat at all yesterday . . . food didn't appeal to me one whit after such a shock. But now it's all catching up with me. As soon as you two leave, I'll probably pig out." She gave her lightly tittering laugh.

Meadow returned in time to hear Laura. "Now don't you worry about us! Go ahead and eat to your heart's content. Sometimes, when life is miserable, eating is one of the few pleasures."

Laura said, "You've got that right! I might have to just have a muffin. Can I offer either one of you one?"

Beatrice wryly patted her stomach. "I've already had more than my fair share this morning. I picked some up for Wyatt and me at the same time I was picking some up for you."

Laura stepped to the side and said, "Do come sit down, both of you." They walked into a lovely living room full of white upholstered furniture and white marbled-topped tables. Beatrice hoped that she wasn't dusty. It seemed that the more construction was done in her house, the dustier things got. And it was a sneaky sort of dust—the kind that you didn't see until it showed up on your clothing later. Or on someone's white furniture.

Laura sank down on a white silk settee, and Beatrice offered her the platter before setting it down on a marble-topped coffee table. The room was beautiful, but seemed somehow sterile to Beatrice, and she wondered if it had been decorated by Gerald or Laura. There were no family pictures up or any art at all. Beatrice knew art wasn't to everyone's decorating taste, but the former art curator in her always missed it when it wasn't there. To her, it offered a lot of insight into the people who lived there.

Somehow, Laura managed to delicately eat a muffin without leaving any crumbs at all on the white furniture. She said, after carefully swallowing a small bite, "Beatrice, I heard that you were at the factory yesterday morning after Wyatt found Gerald. I'm sure that must have been such a shock for him."

Beatrice said, "He is very sorry about your loss. He had a lot of respect for Gerald. I drove over to meet up with Wyatt as soon as he told me what had happened."

Laura looked sadly down at the last bite of her muffin. "And I was asleep the whole time! I feel rather guilty about that. I hadn't been sleeping very well over the last week, and I suppose it just caught up with me all at once. I didn't even wake up when Gerald got up to get ready to walk over to the office and I never slept during that. I feel terrible that I wasn't with him."

Meadow said, "Now, Laura, you know that you shouldn't feel guilty in the slightest! Gerald certainly wouldn't have wanted you there with him. There was a dangerous person in the building—who knows what could have happened? He would have wanted you safe in your bed, exactly where you were."

Laura sighed. "Yes, you're right. It was just bad timing, that's all. Although not out of the ordinary for me to have insomnia.

I haven't slept very well for my entire *life*. It's ironic that the one night I'm finally able to catch up on my rest and sleep in a little is the time when Gerald needed me the most. Meadow, I'm sure Ramsay must have told you how he rang the bell and *rang* the bell. I didn't even hear it until he'd probably rung ten times. I think he must have been about to give up."

Meadow shook her head. "He told me no such thing. Don't you worry your head about this. All Ramsay thinks is that you are a hard sleeper. Our son, Ash, is the same exact way. Why, I've always said that when Ash was a child, Ramsay and I could jump on his bed like a trampoline if we'd wanted and he wouldn't have even stirred."

Beatrice said wryly, "Although hopefully that will change soon."

Laura gave her that beaming smile again, "That's right! With the new baby. With any luck, when the little one cries, Ash won't sleep through it every night or else Piper will be exhausted." She turned again to Meadow. "And thank you for making me feel better. I think it was those guilty feelings about not being there for Gerald that killed my appetite yesterday."

Meadow said, "You need to be tempted by more baked goods, that's all. Goodness knows, the platter Beatrice brought is fairly groaning with them."

Laura obediently picked up a buttermilk biscuit.

Meadow raised a hand. "Now hold on. You can't compromise when eating one of June Bug's biscuits—you need to go all the way with it. I'll run it to the kitchen and heat it up and put a little butter on it."

Laura handed her the biscuit in a napkin and Meadow hurried off with it.

Laura shook her head with a smile. "She's very kind. Both of you are. To tell you the truth, I can hardly believe that Gerald is gone. It feels more like he's just over at the office, working hard, as usual."

"When you're married a long time and you lose someone, it's hard for the reality of it to hit you," said Beatrice. Laura looked at her curiously and Beatrice continued, "I lost my first husband, Piper's father, when Piper was a teenager. It was a rough time for both of us."

Laura said, "Oh, I'm so sorry. It really must have been. And you're absolutely right—Gerald and I have had a wonderful marriage. Of course, it was a second marriage for both of us, but it's been a fairly long one. We loved each other. More than that, we *depended* on each other since he and I sort of balanced each other out."

"That's wonderful. That's ideally what marriage should be like, isn't it?" asked Beatrice. Laura either must not be aware of Gerald's infidelities, or else she was a marvelous actress.

"It is," said Laura with a decisive nod. "He was all work, very serious. And I tried to inject some levity into our lives. Our marriage wasn't perfect, but it worked. Now, with Wyatt's help, I want to plan a funeral service for Gerald that really celebrates his life. I want it all—a horn section, a full choir, the works."

Beatrice smiled at her. "I'm sure that will be lovely. And what a nice way of thinking of the service—as a celebration."

"Yes, because the poor man didn't give himself a chance to celebrate himself often," said Laura.

Meadow joined them with the biscuit now residing on a plate and with a dollop of jam on the side and a glass of milk. "I brought the jam just in case you wanted to add a little punch to the biscuit," she said. Then she said, "I'm sorry, I totally interrupted you, Laura. You were saying that Gerald didn't really celebrate himself?"

"That's exactly right. He was always working so hard." She paused. "Did you know that there were offers for the business? Gerald and the business were really being courted."

Beatrice asked, "What did you think about that?"

"Oh, of course I thought Gerald should be flattered—that the interest from the business community was a testament to his hard work and how wonderful his business was. Mark was all for selling it," she said with a shrug.

Meadow said, "*Mark* was? But Mark seems like he's always so engaged with Dappled Hills Pimento. He's just like his dad, always working."

Laura nodded ruefully. "That he is. But he's also a businessman, through and through. I don't think he has the same loyalty to the company that Gerald did. When he heard a good offer, he tried to persuade Gerald that the time was right to sell."

"But you didn't think so?" asked Beatrice.

Laura shook her head. "No. Dappled Hills Pimento was Gerald's whole life. I couldn't imagine him at home all day. I mean . . . what would he *do*? He wasn't the type of man to sit around and read all day. And he wasn't a bridge player. No, he needed that company, and I didn't want to see him sell it. Gerald was against selling it anyway, so it wasn't going to go any farther."

Meadow said in her typical blunt way, "Wow, I bet that caused some tension in the family. So some people wanted Gerald to sell and some didn't? I can't imagine Mark was very happy with his dad over that."

Laura waved her hand in the air dismissively. "It was just business. Nothing personal. Mark and Gerald argued a lot anyway, because in so many ways they were a lot alike. They were both very intense men. And that's what you do when you're around someone who's just like you—you argue. Anyway, it's not like the family didn't have rifts already." She raised an eyebrow and gave them a mysterious look that prompted them to ask.

Meadow took the bait. "Not Joan?"

It was a good guess, considering that Joan was the only child who hadn't been directly mentioned so far.

Laura nodded coyly. "Joan was always difficult. I could tell when Gerald had visited with her from his demeanor. He'd come home all stiff and grouchy and snap everyone's heads off."

Beatrice said, "Oh, I'm sorry to hear that. I didn't know."

Laura shrugged. "Why would you? It only really happened in private. In public, Joan always put up an act and behaved like the loving daughter. It was always over money, of course."

This made Beatrice raise her own eyebrows. She'd already heard about tension between Joan and her dad, but Joan had indicated that it had other causes.

"Over money?" asked Beatrice.

Laura rolled her eyes. "That and other things. I wouldn't be at all surprised if Joan mentioned to both of y'all that she still held a grudge against Gerald for spending so much time at work when she was a child. I mean, really? She benefitted from all that hard work for many years. Joan was never one to forgive and forget. As I mentioned, Gerald's work was everything to him. Joan might have expressed a little gratitude that her father had made a very comfortable life for her with all of his hard work. Instead, she's been inclined to blame him for all sorts of hateful things, among them her mother's death. I mean, Gerald wasn't driving the *car*. Her mother should have planned things better and not gone out in the dark in bad weather if she wasn't a good driver."

This seemed really harsh, but Beatrice and Meadow both nodded, careful not to look at each other.

"Anyway, I'm sure that Joan is feeling guilty," said Laura with not a small amount of smugness.

Meadow's eyes were huge. "Over what?" She seemed to be expecting Laura to say that Joan had murdered her father. Beatrice knew, with Joan being a quilter, that Meadow would fiercely defend her.

"Over the fact that they had a rousing argument the day before Gerald died," said Laura. "Joan wanted her father to sell the business, too. Naturally! She wanted a handout and that would have been a great way to get it." She shrugged again. "I'm not sure what else they squabbled about since I left the room. I was sick and tired of hearing about it, to tell you the truth. Always the same old song and dance."

Beatrice said, "I'm so sorry to hear this. I'm sure Joan feels terrible about it."

Meadow said, "And she didn't have a chance to make up with him before he died? How awful!"

Laura said, "That's the thing, isn't it? We always think we have more time to say that we're sorry later on. Then one day, time runs completely out."

Chapter Ten

After that, the conversation turned to more pleasant topics. Laura could be a very lively hostess, and she seemed to go on automatic pilot and, despite her grief, engage them in conversation. When she asked more questions about the upcoming baby and Meadow showed absolutely no signs of ending the conversation, Beatrice finally pulled her out of there so that Laura could have a few minutes of peace before Wyatt arrived.

They got into Meadow's car and Meadow said, "That was quite the visit. Gosh! I never knew that there was so much going on under the surface in that family."

Beatrice clutched the door again since Meadow again didn't seem inclined to be focused on the road. "I guess all families have undercurrents that no one guesses at, but theirs seems to have a lot more going on than most."

Meadow said, "I've never really understood Laura, I'll admit. Maybe that's because she presents a particular image to the world, and it's hard to get past the image. I mean, she always looks so perfect—her clothes are perfect, she's the perfect hostess. Even her makeup was perfect, and she's been crying."

"*Has* she been crying?" asked Beatrice, a note of surprise in her voice.

"Well, I *suppose* she has," said Meadow, now sounding a lot less-certain. "With a shock like that, you'd think that you'd burst into tears. But maybe it wasn't that sort of marriage."

"The way that Laura put it, they had a very good marriage," said Beatrice.

"Yes, but marriages don't all work the same way. Like Ramsay's and my marriage—we've been married for so long that we complete each other's sentences or maybe we actually even know what each other is going to say before we say it. We have a lot of jokes that just the two of us understand. But we can exasperate each other like nobody else, too," said Meadow, speeding off down the mountain road.

Beatrice said uneasily, "Slow down a bit, Meadow."

Meadow did. She continued, "And then there's you and Wyatt. Y'all haven't been married very long, and you're just so sweet together."

"Are we?" asked Beatrice with a smile. Wyatt, she suspected, was the sweetest part of the equation. He could always make her feel special.

"You know you're adorable. So tender with each other! But I get the feeling that Laura and Gerald had a rather complex marriage. More so than either of ours."

Beatrice said, "Gerald ran his own business, which kept him at the office for long hours, of course. And then I think that wealth can also create its own complications. And I'm not sure how well Laura got along with Gerald's adult children."

"It would have been tricky, for sure." Meadow paused. "This is bad to say, but I've often wondered what the attraction was there for Laura. I mean, Gerald wasn't exactly the most romantic guy in the world. Like Laura said, his whole world was his business. He wasn't going to be quoting sonnets or writing her love poetry."

Beatrice chuckled, "Is that a normal part of twenty-first century courtship?"

"Well, Ramsay wrote me poetry," said Meadow.

"That, I believe," said Beatrice. Ramsay, if he were in a perfect world, would much prefer to be sitting around reading dusty volumes of fiction and writing poetry and short stories than doing police work and chasing down criminals. "So what do you think the attraction for Laura was?"

Meadow said, "It's hard to imagine it was Gerald's looks. Oh, he was a nice-enough looking man, but he rarely smiled. I hate to say it, but Laura likes her lifestyle. I think it was, in a way, a very businesslike marriage."

Beatrice said, "What kind of relationship do Gerald's kids have with Laura? It sounded like Joan didn't have a very good one, at any rate."

Meadow said, "It sure sounded like Laura wasn't very impressed with Joan. I can't understand that. Joan is terrific! I've always enjoyed talking with her at quilt shows."

That was the thing—Meadow was never going to speak poorly of a quilting sister. Joan could be a total reprobate, and Meadow would be completely blind to it.

"What about Mark?" asked Beatrice.

Meadow said, "I don't think Mark and Laura are *close*, of course. I mean, I didn't see Laura hanging out in town with either Joan or Mark. But I always had the impression that Laura respected Mark. After all, he was following in Gerald's footsteps and was quite a good businessman."

"Although, apparently he wanted his father to sell the business," said Beatrice thoughtfully.

Meadow shrugged and looked over at Beatrice, which made Beatrice hold on even tighter to the door. "But what do we know? Maybe Mark was right, and it was the perfect time to sell and to the perfect buyer."

"Laura indicated that Joan wanted her father to sell the business to help her with her own financial problems," said Beatrice. "And Colleen mentioned that Joan frequently asked her father for money."

Meadow said, "I think that's completely fabricated on Laura's part. I've never seen any hint at all that Joan is destitute. She's a nurse and nurses make a nice living. Besides, Joan doesn't exactly live a glamorous life. I've been by her house before, and it was quite modest."

Beatrice said, "I wonder if Laura really wanted Gerald to hold onto the business."

Meadow said, "Well, she said it was his whole life. I guess she wanted to keep him happy. Otherwise, what on earth was he going to do all day but mope around the house and be underfoot? Nobody wants a bored and unhappy retired husband hanging around."

Beatrice nodded, but suspected it was a more complicated marriage than Meadow thought. Was it possible that Laura knew about Gerald's affairs? She didn't seem like a naïve woman. If so, what kept her quiet about them? Was it just that she was devoted to their marriage, no matter what? Could it all be that Laura was used to her comfortable lifestyle and was happy to look the other way?

Her thoughts were interrupted by Meadow, still chatting blithely away. "So if that works out, I'll just bring you by my house first."

Beatrice blinked at her. "*Your* house? I thought you were taking me right back home."

Meadow hooted a laugh. "You haven't listened to a word I said, have you?"

"Guilty," said Beatrice with a sigh. "Sorry. I've just had a lot on my brain lately."

"Well, don't you worry about it. I've been just the same way—head in the clouds. All I can think about is that precious grandbaby. Ramsay had to call my name three times the other day before I broke free of my happy little daydream! All I was saying was that I wanted to show you the darling baby blanket that I finished. I started describing it to you, but it really does have to be seen in the flesh. Can you pop by for a few minutes?" asked Meadow.

Beatrice said, "I think that should be all right. We're having more work done in the afternoon, and I'm going to give Wyatt a break for a bit. But there's nothing going on right now. I probably should be finishing up that diaper bag. Maybe looking at your finished project will help to inspire me."

Meadow passed by Beatrice's house on the way, and she confirmed that there was no unexpected work truck parked in front of their house. She did spot Noo-noo keeping watch out the front window. The little dog saw her, and her ears perked up, and drooped again as she passed by the house. Beatrice decided that she'd have to take her on a little walk when she got back.

Meadow's house was an old barn which had been lovingly renovated. It was a beautiful space with soaring ceilings festooned with colorful hanging quilts, hardwood floors that had been scavenged from a local mill when it had closed, and an assortment of quirkily uncoordinated furniture from various family members who had long since passed away. It was a place to feel comfortable in, most of all with the smell of cooking frequently lingering around the house. Although, it sounded as if, lately Meadow hadn't been doing a whole lot of cooking besides the meal for Laura.

Boris bounded up to meet them, and Meadow plopped on the floor to let the huge dog give her kisses. "Boris! I missed you, too. Remember, you can't jump on company." The last was said in a warning voice. Somehow, Boris had recently gotten into a jumping habit that he hadn't yet displayed. Because of his tremendous size, he'd nearly taken Beatrice down the last time he'd enthusiastically greeted her.

Boris, although Beatrice usually didn't credit him with nearly the intelligence of her corgi, seemed to understand Meadow, and with great restraint walked meekly over to Beatrice and bumped her hand with his massive head. Beatrice rewarded him by scratching him behind the ears and then rubbing his belly when he ecstatically flopped over.

Meadow was talking as she walked back to the master bedroom to get the blanket. "It's the cutest little quilt! I think Posy stocked the fabric just for you and me. Have you noticed that a good portion of the fabrics now have baby themes? Anyway, I thought this one might grow with the baby for a little while."

She returned, carrying a plush quilt with plaid squares and dotted squares interspersed with squares of sweet-looking animals—a cute deer, a fetching fox, a little bunny.

"It's adorable," said Beatrice sincerely. "And I think you're right that the baby will enjoy it for a while."

Meadow beamed at her. "Or, when the baby finally outgrows it, maybe it will be time for a *new* baby."

Beatrice said dryly, "One baby at a time, Meadow. I don't think I can handle the excitement of thinking about two." She reached out a hand and smoothed it over the little quilt. "It's so soft. I love this fabric."

"It's organic cotton, believe it or not, but it's *so* soft. I wanted to make sure to get something very natural for the baby to let his or her little skin breathe," said Meadow.

The door opened, and Ramsay came in. He gave them a weary grin. "How are things going on the baby front?"

Beatrice said, "I think we're all set for the little one. Now we just have to wait for the birth."

Ramsay chuckled and said, "Well, it's good to hear that at least *something* is going well."

Meadow made a face. "Don't tell me the investigation isn't going well. That murderer has got to be tracked down before he strikes again."

Ramsay said patiently, "We're doing everything we can, Meadow. But there's not a lot of evidence, unfortunately."

"Did you find out his cause of death?" asked Beatrice.

Ramsay nodded. "It was an overdose of sleeping pills, I'm afraid. Someone must have known Gerald's routine pretty well. Whoever did this slipped into his office and put a slew of sleeping pills into his coffee."

Beatrice frowned. "But wouldn't Gerald have been able to tell by the taste that something was wrong? Shouldn't it have tasted bad enough for him to simply pour it out?"

Ramsay said, "You'd think so, but apparently the bitter taste of the coffee was strong enough to mask it. Or maybe Gerald was distracted by his work and didn't really pay attention to his drink. At any rate, I've heard that he liked his coffee very strong and very dark, which probably helped the killer out."

Meadow put her hands on her hips. "Are you saying that someone lurked outside Gerald's office, waiting for him to be distracted so that they could slip sleeping pills into his coffee?"

"I'm afraid so," said Ramsay.

Beatrice said, "Did Gerald take sleeping pills normally?"

"From what I've been able to find out from his family, he did have a prescription on autofill for a year or more when he was having trouble sleeping after being prescribed some other medication. But he didn't use them after the first couple of times. From all accounts, Gerald Carpenter was the kind of person who liked to have full control at all times—he didn't like having a pill knock him out," said Ramsay.

Meadow was still dwelling on the killer's lurking. "I can't believe that someone just hung around waiting for a chance to doctor his coffee!"

Ramsay said, "Well, that's what happened. But anyone who had a good idea of Gerald's habits could easily have figured out what to do. Gerald went to the office extremely early—he was frequently there at five o'clock in the morning, hours before anyone else. When he arrived, the first thing he did was make himself a pot of coffee."

Beatrice asked, "Was this coffeemaker in the company breakroom?"

"Nope. It was his very own stash in his office. There was a separate coffeemaker in the employee breakroom, but it wasn't tampered with. At any rate, he had an established routine, according to his current assistant. He went in, made himself coffee, and then he started looking at work and emails. Then, usually about an hour after he came in, he'd go to a vending machine and get himself a snack. He liked to get a Snickers bar."

"Not the healthiest of breakfasts," said Meadow, making a face.

"Regardless, it's what he did," said Ramsay with a shrug.

Beatrice asked, "Now the *vending machine* surely wasn't in his private office, was it?"

"No, you're right, that was in the breakroom for the employees. So he did get up from his office and go to another room," said Ramsay.

Beatrice said, "Leaving behind an unmonitored cup of coffee."

"Exactly. And it was a regular routine—to the point that it was something of a family joke when I asked Mark about it," said Ramsay.

Meadow looked sternly at Ramsay, "Surely you don't think that his family had something to do with his death."

Beatrice could tell that Meadow was still thinking of Joan and the complete impossibility of a quilter being involved in a violent crime.

Ramsay sighed and said, "Now, Meadow, you know that the police have to look at everyone. Family traditionally are important suspects. After all, they would know Gerald's routine best. They'd also have access to the sleeping pills."

"Wouldn't other people know his routine, too?" demanded Meadow.

Ramsay said, "Sure. That's something we're working on now. Gerald was close to people outside of the family, and they certainly could have found out his routine. They also may have had access to his house from time to time."

The doorbell rang, and Boris went berserk.

"Boris!" said Ramsay sternly, but Boris would not be quieted. He bounded over to the front door, barking wildly.

Meadow said, "I'll get it."

She hurried over there, grabbing Boris's collar and opening the door. Beatrice waved a hand in greeting at the woman standing there. She couldn't remember her name, but knew that she went to their church and was friendly with Meadow. Apparently, she'd come by to show Meadow her vacation pictures. With Boris still wildly out of control, Meadow abandoned the house with her friend, choosing to sit out on the patio instead as Boris ran from window to window, trying to get a better glimpse of Meadow.

Beatrice hesitated. She wanted to help Ramsay to solve the case, but she also wanted to protect any conversations she'd had that were supposed to be confidential. She decided to try and find out exactly what Ramsay knew, especially now that Meadow was safely out of earshot.

"Ramsay, thinking back to the matter of the sleeping pills and having access to them, is it possible that Gerald was having affairs? And that those women might have been able to know about his sleeping pills and have taken some of them?"

Ramsay's eyebrows shot up so high that they were almost on the top of his head. "You're more in the know than I thought you'd be."

Beatrice said wryly, "I wish I *didn't* know. But people have entrusted me with their secrets because I'm sort of a proxy to Wyatt, I guess. I don't want to divulge what they've told me, but I wanted to make sure that you were aware of it."

"Thanks for that. I found out by following a few leads in the family. Apparently, family members were not completely unaware of Gerald's activities," said Ramsay.

"Including Laura?" Beatrice asked slowly.

Ramsay shook his head. "It seems as if Laura knew nothing about his affairs. Maybe it's more that she was determined not to. But both of his children mentioned that Laura would leave town occasionally to visit family and that their father could have hosted women who might have seen the sleeping pills in the medicine cabinet."

Beatrice said, "That definitely makes it a little harder to find out who murdered Gerald."

Ramsay said in a tired voice, "Tell me about it. Plus the fact that the sleeping pills were also at the office."

"At the *office*?"

"That's right. Gerald had gone to the drugstore one day during working hours to pick up some over the counter medicine for a head cold. While he was there, the pharmacist told him that he had a prescription to pick up. The sleeping pills were on auto-refill, so Gerald paid for them at the same time and took everything back to the office, where I suppose he promptly forgot about the medicine," said Ramsay.

"So someone who worked at the factory could have seen them and taken them for later," said Beatrice.

"Exactly. Although I'm not sure who would have known about them besides maybe his assistant. Someone would have had to have gone snooping through his desk and come across them. And the thing is that Gerald had a very organized desk and file system. The pills probably stood out like a sore thumb."

Beatrice asked, "I know you didn't want us to mention anything about Gerald being tied up, so I didn't want to say anything while Meadow was around. Do you have any ideas why Gerald would have been tied up like that? It seems really unnecessary to me if the sleeping pills were how he was murdered."

Ramsay said, "Well, the forensics guys said that he was tied up sometime after he'd been drugged with the sleeping pills. They guessed that maybe the murderer was worried that the pills would be slow-acting and that Gerald might realize what was happening to him and would call for the police or an ambulance."

"That would have obviously messed up their plan," said Beatrice. "So the ropes were brought in to keep Gerald from getting help. And his stomach was pumped?"

"Exactly. So maybe the murderer waited for the drugs to take effect and then surprised Gerald by tying him up and completely incapacitating him until the pills knocked him out and later killed him. I guess it was easier than disabling his office phone and trying to get his cell phone away from him." Then Ramsay grimaced. "Do you mind if I abruptly change the subject? I think I've talked about this case a little too much. Tell me what you're reading right now."

Beatrice smiled at him. "Wyatt and I are reading the same book again."

"Ah, your Wyatt and Beatrice book club is still in session?" asked Ramsay with a grin. "I thought maybe it was going to disband after the last unsuccessful read."

"Well, I think we discovered that I'm not as much of a fan of reading biographies of long-dead theologians as he is. Although, they were excellent sleep aids for me during nights when I was having trouble falling asleep. But it was my turn to come up with a title this time and I picked one that I thought might appeal to both of us. *All the Light We Cannot See.* I figured that maybe the historical aspect of the story might make it more interesting for Wyatt," said Beatrice.

Ramsay nodded his approval. "That's a very thoughtful choice." He chuckled. "Maybe it will inspire Wyatt to try a little harder to come up with a better pick next time."

"Let's hope so! Although the thought behind his choices were very sweet. They were books that had heavily influenced the way he saw life and religion and helped make him the minister he is today. I was interested in reading them to find out more about Wyatt, but I suppose that I'm just not used to reading those types of texts. At any rate, I managed to limp through them, and I did get a little more insight into Wyatt's thought processes."

Meadow, who had wrapped up with her friend, came back inside. Boris leaped on her and licked her face and neck as if to apologize for his earlier behavior, and she hugged him around his big neck in forgiveness while futilely trying to keep her face away from Boris's tongue.

"Oh, Beatrice," said Meadow with a groan, "Now you're going to inspire Ramsay to get on another spousal book club kick. I don't think I can handle it. All of the stuff that he suggests we read is really depressing. I want something *uplifting*. I want something that can make me escape."

Ramsay said, "But those books I picked could help you escape, too."

"Escape? No, those books took me to a place that I needed to escape *from*. Yes, I armchair-traveled, but not to a happy place," said Meadow with a shudder.

"What were some of these books?" asked Beatrice, a smile pulling at her lips.

"Awful things!" spat Meadow. "Something called *The Street*, for one."

"I think she's referring to McCarthy's *The Road*," said Ramsay with a chuckle.

Beatrice groaned. "You didn't. That's not exactly a Meadow book, Ramsay."

"It certainly wasn't!" said Meadow indignantly.

Ramsay said, "But you said that you wanted a page-turner. And that's definitely a page-turner."

"Only because I was trying to skip ahead and see if the dad and his little guy survived the book! I'm still having nightmares about that one," said Meadow, making a face.

Beatrice said, "There must be some other ones that weren't that bad."

Meadow shook her head and Ramsay said, "I thought you enjoyed *Bleak House*."

"I enjoying *finishing* the book. And Dickens always writes amazing characters. But how could one really *enjoy* a book called *Bleak House*?" demanded Meadow.

Ramsay said, "But Beatrice, we swung back from my two picks with a vengeance when Meadow's turns came up to choose."

Beatrice winced. "I can only imagine."

Meadow said, "I couldn't handle anything emotionally draining so I found two of the frothiest romances I could possibly find."

"They didn't even have a plot," said Ramsay, groaning in remembrance.

Meadow grinned. "Which was entirely necessary to recover from your book choices."

Beatrice tried to be diplomatic. "Maybe you could find a little common ground. Have either of you read the Harry Potter series?"

Meadow and Ramsay looked at each other and then shook their heads. Ramsay said, "It kind of pains me to admit it, but no. And we didn't see the films, either."

Beatrice said, "They have a lot of humor and fun in them but also have some dark moments. They might make for a good compromise for you both."

Ramsay said, "Thanks for the recommendation. There has to be common ground somewhere between the books I read and the ones Meadow does."

Meadow said, "That might actually work for us. I just couldn't read anything really sad right when we're about to meet our darling grandbaby. If I left it up to Ramsay, I'd be reading *Jude the Obscure* or something."

"I don't think there's much chance for me to read something right now, unfortunately." Ramsay's eyes were sad. "But maybe in the next couple of weeks."

"No, there's definitely not time for you to read," agreed Meadow. "You have to restore law and order to Dappled Hills so that our grandchild has a safe place to play."

Beatrice said with a smile, "Now, Meadow. You know that Dappled Hills is a safe place ninety-nine percent of the time. What's happening right now is an anomaly and Ramsay is on top of it."

Beatrice's phone rang and Meadow jumped. "Is it Piper? Is it time?"

Chapter Eleven

Ramsay rolled his eyes dramatically. "I'd better grab that snack that I'm home for and head back on my way. Good to see you, Beatrice."

He wandered over to the pantry as Beatrice glanced at her phone. "It's Wyatt, Meadow." She picked up. "Hey there."

"Hi," said Wyatt. "Just wanted to check in with you real quick and see if you can handle a change of plan."

"Oh?"

"After I visit with Laura Carpenter about the service, I'm going to need to drive to Lenoir. We have a member of the congregation who has been admitted to the hospital there. Would you be all right to meet with Len when he comes to work? And what should we do about Noo-noo?"

Beatrice said, "Absolutely. I can be there. I'll probably take Noo-noo over to the Patchwork Cottage, since that worked so well before."

"Do you think she could even go into the backyard?" asked Wyatt.

"I'd like to think so, but I think her ears are so big that she'd be bothered by the racket even outside. Posy didn't seem to mind at all—I'll just pop Noo-noo over there."

Wyatt said ruefully, "I'm not sure that Posy *would* say something, even if she did mind."

"I'd agree with you there. But she actually mentioned that Noo-noo was something of a draw for the customers, so I think she really is fine with it. Of course, I'll ask her again," said Beatrice.

They wrapped up the call. Meadow was standing there looking a little pink. "Sorry about that," she said. "I'm starting to get jumpy about the baby getting born. I just know that I'm going to get that call when I'm in the middle of a dental visit or stuck doing something else that I can't get away from. I'm just so excited that I don't want to miss anything."

Beatrice said firmly, "Piper and Ash are a hundred percent prepared. They have everything they need for the baby, they have a plan, and Piper has a packed suitcase. If the baby came right now, it's not too early. Everything is going to be perfectly fine."

Meadow said quickly, "Oh, I know, I know. I'm being silly. So the phone call—let me guess. You're needing to hang out at home this afternoon."

"Which is fine. I wanted to wrap up the diaper bag for Piper, anyway. And then I could read my book for a while."

Meadow said, "You can read with all that noise going on?"

"I put some headphones on and play soft music on my phone. It works pretty well. Besides, we *really* want this construction to be finished, so it's worth it to me so that we can actually use our kitchen again. I'll just run by the Patchwork Cottage and check in with Posy before dropping Noo-noo off."

Meadow said, "Well, if it's not a good time for Posy, then *I* will take Noo-noo."

Beatrice knew that hanging out with Boris wouldn't be Noo-noo's most favorite choice. Boris grinned his goofy grin at her. "Thanks for that! I'll let you know in case it's not convenient for Posy." She started for the door.

Meadow said, "Don't you want me to drive you home? You don't have your car here, remember?"

Beatrice had had quite enough of Meadow's driving for one day and was still feeling remotely carsick from the curves Meadow had taken so quickly. "No, I think the walk will do me good. But thanks."

The walk home was very pleasant, and Beatrice enjoyed stretching her legs. Under the trees, it was shady enough to feel cool. There were flowering bushes and a dappled light shone through the leaves overhead. Beatrice used the time to decompress before getting home. Despite what she'd said to Meadow, she didn't really enjoy being at home when the counters and cabinets were being replaced, headphones or not.

Noo-noo greeted her at the door as she let herself in. Wyatt had already headed off to see Laura Carpenter and Gerald's children, but Beatrice saw that he'd cleaned up the house before he'd left and smiled.

She had a little leftover quiche (warming it up in the microwave that was currently residing on the back wall of the living room) and then picked up the phone and called Posy at the Patchwork Cottage.

Posy answered, sounding distracted. "Oh, hi, Beatrice."

"Everything all right there?"

Posy said slowly, "It's fine, thanks. I'm just a little worried about Salome because she didn't show up this morning to open the shop. It's just really not like her—she's never really even late for anything. I wouldn't have even known about it except that a customer ended up calling me and asking why the shop wasn't open."

"Is she all right?" asked Beatrice. "Have you heard from her?"

Posy's voice was concerned. "She isn't answering her phone, and unfortunately, I don't have her sister's number. Usually, Carla takes Salome's daughter, Jenna, to school and then goes straight to work."

Beatrice said, "I can run by there, if you like, just to check and make sure that she's all right?"

Posy sounded relieved. "Could you? I'm sure she's probably fine—maybe she came down with a virus or something. I'd have called Ramsay to run by, but I know that he has his hands full right now. And I didn't want to leave the shop." She quickly gave Beatrice the address.

"Absolutely. I'll go straight over there." Beatrice glanced at her watch. She still had plenty of time before Len was supposed to arrive, and Noo-noo could stay at the house while she was gone. She rubbed the little dog's head before grabbing her keys and heading to the car.

She used her phone's GPS to drive over to the brick ranch where Salome lived with her sister, Carla, and her child. The yard and house were tidy, and there were cheerful flowerbeds at the mailbox and near the front of the house. Beatrice hurried up the walkway and rang the doorbell. She waited, listening, and then rang it again. She noticed that there was still a car left in the driveway. Then she noticed that the door was very slightly ajar.

Not wanting to simply walk in, she knocked loudly on the door and waited. No response. Tentatively, she pushed the door open.

Beatrice cleared her throat and stepped inside. "Salome? It's Beatrice Thompson. I'm just checking on you. Posy asked me if I could run by."

She listened again and heard nothing. Taking a deep breath, she walked a little further in and called out again, "Salome? It's Beatrice. Is everything okay?"

Nothing.

Hesitantly, Beatrice walked even further into the dimly-lit house. "Salome?"

She walked into the kitchen and stopped short. There, on the floor, lay Salome with a cast-iron frying pan next to her.

Chapter Twelve

Beatrice called Ramsay first, right after she'd checked for Salome's non-existent pulse with shaking hands. Then she stepped outside and waited by her car.

Ramsay was there within a couple of minutes, and the state police, still in town investigating Gerald's death, were just behind him.

"In the kitchen," said Beatrice quietly as the police entered the house and secured the scene.

A few minutes later, Ramsay came grimly back out. He shook his head. "You and Wyatt have had a bad week. I'm sorry, Beatrice."

Beatrice shook her head and cleared her throat. "I'm sorry too, but mostly for Salome. She didn't deserve this. And now, there's a little girl who will be growing up without her mother."

Ramsay flipped open his small notebook and sighed. "Okay if I ask you some questions? Just while everything is fresh on your mind?"

"Of course," said Beatrice. She carefully moved her neck from side to side to try to get some of the tension out of it. As she did, she noticed several of the neighbors had come out of their homes to see what was happening.

Ramsay said, "What made you decide to come by here this morning? I know Meadow acts like everyone who quilts is her very best friend, but I thought that neither of you knew Salome very well."

"You're right—we didn't. Lately, with Salome working part-time in the Patchwork Cottage and with Meadow and me doing a lot of quilting for the baby, we've had the opportunity to see her a little more. But under ordinary circumstances, I wouldn't have come by her house. Posy called me when Salome didn't show up for work this morning."

Ramsay nodded. "I'll have to speak with Posy, then. Did she happen to mention what time Salome should have been there?"

"Well, the shop opens at ten o'clock, and Posy said that Salome was supposed to open. I'm sure Posy would have probably expected Salome there a little earlier than opening time to make sure the shop was tidy and the cash register ready to go. At any rate, a customer apparently called Posy to ask why the Patchwork Cottage was still closed. I called Posy to see if Noo-noo could hang out at the shop while the construction was going on, and she told me she was worried about Salome," said Beatrice.

Ramsay asked, "Do you know where Salome's sister and her daughter are?"

Beatrice shook her head slowly. "No. I'm sure Carla is going to be devastated. I'm not sure where she works. Posy said that usually her sister left the house earlier than Salome to go to work and drop Jenna off at preschool for her." She swallowed. "Her poor family."

"We'll find out who did this," said Ramsay grimly.

Beatrice said, "I just can't figure out why someone would feel they had to murder Salome. She didn't seem to really know anything when I talked with her about Gerald's death." She paused and then said slowly, "There was one thing. But I'm not sure that I didn't just imagine it."

Ramsay said, "I'd like to hear it, regardless, if you don't mind."

"I don't know whether she told you or not, but Salome indicated that she'd been at Gerald's office the morning he was killed," said Beatrice.

Ramsay's eyebrows shot up. "No, she didn't tell me anything about that. Did she go inside the office?"

"No. At least, that's not what she told me. She said that she hung around for a few minutes but didn't see Gerald's car there. Then she said that she'd driven away."

Ramsay frowned. "That's kind of odd. His car was definitely parked there, but maybe it wasn't in the spot that Salome expected it to be in."

Beatrice said, "Or maybe something else happened that made Salome drive off. Maybe she saw someone else there. When she realized that she wasn't going to have a private audience with Gerald, she decided to leave and try again another time."

Ramsay asked intently, "Did she *say* that she had seen someone there?"

"No, but when I asked her if she had, she didn't immediately answer me," said Beatrice.

"So maybe she did see someone. The killer. And now, sud-denly, Salome is dead, too," said Ramsay, looking frustrated. "But why wouldn't she have told me—or you—what she'd seen?"

"Maybe she wasn't totally sure what she'd seen, and she was still trying to process it. Maybe she was afraid of implicating someone when she wasn't positive they were responsible. Or maybe she considered trying to make money from her knowl-edge." Beatrice shrugged and said sadly, "As you mentioned ear-lier, desperate times call for desperate measures."

Ramsay said, "I had a quick question for you—just one thread we're following in our investigation. I'd ask Meadow, but she absolutely explodes whenever I suggest that a quilter could possibly have anything to do with a murder investigation."

Beatrice smiled. "Then you must be asking about Joan."

Ramsay grinned. "How did you guess? I don't know how well you know Joan, but we've found reason to suspect that she might have had some financial concerns. Do you know anything about those? Is she a big spender?"

Beatrice said, "Unfortunately, I don't, I'm sorry." She hesi-tated. "I have heard that second-hand, but you and I might be hearing it from the same source—Laura. I don't think that she and Joan have the best relationship, though. And I don't person-ally know anything about Joan's financial affairs. I'm *starting* to know her better, but not enough to know anything about her fi-nancial situation."

"Got it. Just one thing we're trying to follow up on," said Ramsay.

One of the state policemen called out to Ramsay, and he closed his notebook. "I'll check back in with you later," he said. "Thanks for this." He walked toward the house and the policeman.

Beatrice turned to walk around to the driver's side of her car and stopped when she saw Joan Carpenter parking her car in front of her.

Joan's car door immediately swung opened, and she hurried toward Beatrice. Her face was white. "What happened?" she asked in a rush.

Beatrice said, "I'm so sorry, Joan. Salome has passed away."

"What?" Her voice broke as she spoke.

"Salome didn't show up this morning at the shop, and Posy asked if I could run by and check on her. When I got here, I . . . found her."

Joan stepped back until she was slumping against Beatrice's car. "Dead! Murdered?" she asked urgently.

"I'm afraid so," said Beatrice.

Joan shook her head and said, "I can't believe it. What's happening around here?" Her voice rose at the end.

More police cars pulled up, and Beatrice said again, "I'm sorry. Here, would you like to sit down in my car for a minute?" Joan was wobbling a little from the shock.

Joan nodded, and they both climbed into the car.

"I can't believe this," she murmured. "Poor Salome. And what's going to happen to her daughter now?"

Beatrice said, "I know. I'm sure Carla will step in, but I feel terrible for them both."

Joan said absently, "And I've just been driving around town doing random errands and meeting with Wyatt while Salome was in trouble at her own home. I wish I'd known."

Beatrice said, "Whatever happened, it was fast. I don't think that Salome suffered at all. I know you'd been looking for her to talk to her when I saw you at the Patchwork Cottage. Were you ever able to catch up with her?"

Joan shook her head. "No. And I feel terrible about that. I wish I'd had the chance to speak with her again." She turned to look through the car window at Salome's house. "We're going to have to do something to help little Jenna." She hesitated and then said, "You probably don't know this, but Jenna was my father's daughter. My half-sister." The last words ended in a sob, and Joan fought to keep control over her emotions.

Beatrice kept her expression very still and said quietly, "I'm so sorry. This must all be so very hard for you."

Joan gave a hard laugh. "No, it *should* have been hard for all of us. Instead, Dad made things a whole lot less-complicated by refusing paternity and then removing Salome from his sight by firing her. We should have been helping Salome out when she needed us instead of denying that her child was part of our family."

"When did you find out about this?" asked Beatrice.

Joan said, "Not immediately. Oh, I'd known that Dad fired Salome. I thought that was outrageous enough on its own. Salome was the perfect assistant for Dad because she was just as organized as he was. She fell right into his methods of filing, saving emails, and scheduling. She made life so much easier for Dad. And then one day, he abruptly fired her. I was flabbergasted."

"Did you ask your father about it?" asked Beatrice.

"Right away. He was very brusque with me and told me not to ask questions about matters I didn't understand and which weren't any of my business. I told him that he was never going to find another Salome—that he was going to end up going through a string of assistants, just like he did before Salome came on board. He'd never been satisfied with any of them. He just growled at me and waved me out of his office," said Joan, rolling her eyes at the memory.

"So you asked Salome," guessed Beatrice.

"Exactly. I was worried about Salome anyway because I knew she was a single mom. I just didn't know that her daughter was my half-sister," said Joan, her voice tight. "I caught up with her here at her sister's house one day and sat down right on that front porch there and asked her if she was doing all right. I told her I was worried about her. That triggered this outpouring of emotion—sadness, fear, worry. She told me that her daughter was Dad's."

Beatrice said softly, "That must have been a terrible shock for you."

Joan gave a strangled laugh. "It was a terrible shock that my father would treat Salome and Jenna that way. It made me see him in a totally different light. I mean, I'd always known that my father was no angel. After all, it was his selfishness and focus on the business that I blamed for my mother's car accident. But for him to cheat on Laura with his own assistant and then deny the child that came as a result of their affair? I was livid."

"Did you approach your father about it?" asked Beatrice.

"I sure did. I left Salome's house and marched straight over to Dad's office. I let him have it. And the whole time he just looked at me with this cold expression on his face. He had no intention of righting any wrongs, I can tell you that," said Joan.

"What did you do then?"

"I called Salome and spoke with her. I felt so guilty by association with my father. She was so sweet and told me not to worry—that her sister had said she could live with her as long as she needed to and that Posy had stepped in and offered her a part-time job while she was looking for an office job. That only made me feel slightly better. I slipped Salome a little money from time to time, but I've been low on funds, myself, so it wasn't as much as I wanted. Her main concern was finding quality childcare for her daughter so that she and Carla could both work," said Joan.

Beatrice said, "That was good of you. It sounds like you've worked hard to redress your father's actions."

Joan snorted. "Not hard enough. Salome was just scraping by. And here Laura is, living high on the hog, not a care in the world." She sighed. "She's going to be living even better, soon, as Dad's widow. She seems to have done well by Dad's will."

"You've met with the lawyer?" asked Beatrice.

"Yes. And Mark is not particularly pleased with the terms of the will. It sounds like Dad was especially generous to Laura. I have to admit that I wouldn't have turned down money from Dad, either—I've made some poor investments in the past few years at an attempt to do day-trading. It didn't go so well. I mean, Dad definitely provided for Mark and me, but not to the extent that he did Laura."

"And Salome's daughter didn't benefit at all, I'm guessing?" asked Beatrice.

"Not a bit," said Joan. She pressed her lips together tightly.

"Does Laura know about Salome?" asked Beatrice.

Joan said, "Who knows? She's never said anything to me about it. Maybe she was happy just to look the other way. After all, if she stayed married to Dad then she was able to live this really comfortable life that she'd gotten used to. But I doubt that *Dad* would have said anything to her about it. He was all about covering up what he'd done and denying Salome anything."

Beatrice said carefully, "Meadow and I stopped by Laura's house this morning and brought her some breakfast before Wyatt went over to meet you all about the service. Laura talked a good deal about your father."

Joan rolled her eyes. "I can only guess what she said. She always acts like the most loyal wife ever and sooo supportive of her husband. And, if you count lip service, she certainly was. But that woman gets on my nerves, and I'm sure I get on hers, too." She paused. "Did she say anything about me?"

Beatrice gave a short nod, and Joan continued with a groan, "Laura always does. She likes to spread around her own version of the truth to everyone she can. And somehow, I always end up being the bad guy in these versions of the truth. The evil Joan who needs money and is selfishly angry at her father for events that took place decades ago."

Beatrice kept quiet, and Joan kept on, "Sorry, it just makes me mad. People believe her, you know. She's a prominent person in town. I think she spreads this stuff so that everyone is distracted from looking at *her* and what she's up to."

Beatrice asked, "What is it that you think she's up to?"

"Well, I sure don't think my dad was the only one in that relationship having affairs. She probably just kept hers under close wraps because she knew Dad wouldn't put up with any public humiliation. He wouldn't have been able to bear it—he was a very proud man," said Joan. She looked back over at Salome's house. "I just don't know if I can believe that Laura could murder Dad and Salome in cold blood. She's calculating in her way, but I don't see her as being a killer."

Beatrice said, "Who do you think *might* have done this?"

Joan blew out a long breath. "I just don't know. All I keep thinking about is that everyone has been acting differently lately. Laura had been even more insipid and fawning whenever Dad was around. I guess I've been stressed out because I knew the truth about Salome's baby and was so disappointed in my father. And then Mark has been different because of his concerns about the business and pressuring Dad into selling it at what he thought was a good time." She hesitated. "Mark and I have always gotten along pretty well. I guess that's because he and I are two totally different kinds of people. But lately, Mark has been really difficult to get along with."

"Stress from the job maybe?" asked Beatrice.

Joan shook her head. "No. I mean, don't get me wrong, the business has been plenty stressful. But the way that Mark has been acting, it's been more like a midlife crisis. By that I just mean a really abrupt change. Some of the things he was doing fit a midlife crisis to a T. He got a new, sportier car. He changed the way he'd been doing his hair and started buying some expensive new clothes."

"Could he have thought that the sale of the business was really going to come through?" asked Beatrice.

"That could be it. But I don't know, it seemed like it was more than that. That was all stuff that was happening on the surface. What made me really raise my eyebrows was when we were together at a family dinner, and Dad reprimanded him for losing his temper at the office a few times that week. I mean—Mark is always cool and collected. I had a hard time believing that he could lose it at the office," said Joan.

"I don't know Mark very well, but I agree that sounds out of character for what I know about him," said Beatrice. "He always does seem very collected."

"And that was one thing that my father always tried to be at the office: the one in control. Dad wanted to always be the one with iron control, especially in front of employees. Although I guess that control slipped when he fired Salome that day. She told me that he'd really yelled at her," said Joan miserably.

Beatrice said, "What's going to happen with Dappled Hills Pimento Cheese now that your dad isn't there to run it? Will Mark step in?"

Joan sighed. "I actually went by there this morning as one of my errands. Mark insisted that the employees needed to work, no matter what happened—that they needed both the money and the routine. I thought we should close up for a couple of days out of respect for Dad, but he wouldn't hear of it. Mark will be in charge of the company now. I suppose he'll finally get his wish and sell it soon. All I know is that he wasn't happy to see me there this morning, showing any kind of interest in the business. He was glad when I left."

"Why do you think that was?" asked Beatrice.

"I'm guessing that he's hoping to sell the company as soon as he can and that he doesn't want anyone else to stand in his way," said Joan with a shrug.

"Would you stand in his way?" asked Beatrice.

Joan gave a short laugh. "Not at all. I've seen what that business did to Dad and I think it's time that we sell it before it consumes Mark, too. Not that Mark ever talks enough to me to actually know what I think about anything. He's too absorbed in the business, just like Dad was. If he'd simply taken the time to ask me, I'd have told him."

Joan sighed. "Thanks for hearing me out again, Beatrice. It seems like all I do is unload on you whenever I see you. I'd better go get ready for work."

Beatrice said goodbye and watched as Joan drove away. She headed slowly back to the Patchwork Cottage.

Chapter Thirteen

Posy's face was hopeful when she saw Beatrice come through the door, but when Beatrice shook her head, it crumpled. "Oh, no," she said, putting her hands to her face. "What happened, Beatrice?'

Beatrice quietly gave her the bad news. Posy's gentle eyes filled with tears. "Oh, that poor girl."

Beatrice reached out to give Posy a hug. Posy hugged her hard and then pulled back. She said with wide eyes, "And you found her. I'm so sorry, Beatrice. Sorry that you had to go through that."

Beatrice shook her head. "It was better this way, Posy. What if Salome's sister and daughter had found her? It would have been so much worse."

Posy said sadly, "I just never thought that something this serious could have happened to her. I figured that maybe she had some car trouble because she drove an old car. Or that maybe she'd had a long night with Jenna keeping her up and had overslept. Or that she was sick or something. I never expected that something like this could have happened."

"What happened?" demanded a crotchety and elderly voice from the sitting area.

Posy's eyes opened wide. She whispered to Beatrice, "Miss Sissy took quite a liking to Salome and Jenna. She's not going to take this well."

Miss Sissy, always spryer than you'd think she'd be, darted toward them. Her wiry hair had mostly come out of the messy bun she always sported, and she looked as if she'd just woken up. Beatrice winced. Miss Sissy could be moody at the best of times but if she was upset then she made *everyone* have a rough day.

Fortunately, Miss Sissy was briefly waylaid by Maisie the shop cat. While she bent over to gently pet the cat, Beatrice hissed to Posy, "I'll trade you. Could you take Noo-noo for the afternoon, and I'll take Miss Sissy?"

Posy quickly said, "You know I'd love to have Noo-noo here. Do you mind taking Miss Sissy? I know that everyone who comes in the shop is going to be talking about Salome and that's not going to be a good distraction for her."

"Absolutely," said Beatrice. "It's no trouble at all."

Except that it did end up being some trouble. Beatrice ran back home to pick up Noo-noo and drop her off at the shop. Then she persuaded a particularly sour and angry Miss Sissy into her car.

"Stay on the road!" barked the old woman as Beatrice headed back home.

"I *am* on the road," said Beatrice through gritted teeth. From the way Miss Sissy drove, the old woman's impression of what constituted the road was decidedly skewed.

Trying to get Miss Sissy's attention off of the road, Beatrice started talking about the kitchen project. "So at some point, Len is coming back over, and you and I can sit outside in the backyard."

Miss Sissy looked suspicious. "Not in the hammock." Her snarl indicated her general mistrust and disregard for the ropy recliner.

"I may get in the hammock, if you won't. But there is a table and chairs out there, too," said Beatrice, trying to sound persuasive. The last thing Posy needed was for Miss Sissy to disapprove of the arrangements and ask to go back to the Patchwork Cottage.

Miss Sissy grunted.

"We could have a picnic out there," suggested Beatrice. Then she pressed her lips together. She couldn't possibly host a picnic on the scale that would be needed for the always-ravenous Miss Sissy with the yogurt, bread, and peanut butter that she knew to be at the house.

Now Miss Sissy had perked up, however. "Yes, a picnic."

Beatrice said slowly, "Okay. The only problem is that there isn't a lot of food in the house because Wyatt and I have been eating a lot of sandwiches since we can't use the kitchen."

Miss Sissy scowled at her, and Beatrice quickly said, "So let's turn around and go by the grocery store. We can pick up things for the picnic and maybe some more paper plates and plastic cups since it's tricky to get to the dishwasher. But nothing that needs heating up!"

Miss Sissy gave her a scornful sideways glance as if she understood completely and didn't need to be reminded what the limitations were. But as soon as they were in the grocery store, Miss Sissy acted as if she were on a timer. She started pulling things off the shelves and out of the refrigerated section and into the cart. Bread, hard-boiled eggs, unusual mustards, charcuteries, and fruit bowls quickly entered the cart along with cereals, pickles, chips, crackers, and other general grocery items.

Beatrice had the feeling that Miss Sissy was not planning on paying for any of the things in the cart. "Now, it's just for the afternoon, Miss Sissy." Because the amount that the old woman had put in the grocery cart indicated that she was planning for the Siege of Leningrad. Or an extended stay at Beatrice's house.

Miss Sissy continued trotting through the store, but only put five or six more items in. They went through the checkout line, and Beatrice winced at the bill's total. At least it was all food that she and Wyatt could eat without heating up. If Miss Sissy didn't plan on eating everything in the next couple of hours.

When they finally pulled up in front of Beatrice's house, there was another unwelcome surprise: Len's truck was in the driveway, idling.

Miss Sissy growled.

Beatrice gave Miss Sissy her keys. "Here you are. If you could take a small bag, I'll get the rest of them."

Miss Sissy, scowling with narrowed eyes at Len, snatched one of the lighter bags out of the car and stomped toward the house.

"The fridge is in the living room!" called out Beatrice. She received a louder growl in response.

Len was getting out of his truck and cocked an eyebrow as his gaze followed Miss Sissy.

Beatrice sighed. "She's a family friend who's had a very difficult day. We're going to try to keep out of your way while you work, although I'll be checking in to see how things are going. I did take our dog somewhere for the afternoon."

Len nodded his head. "Probably a good idea. Reckon the dog wouldn't like the sound of construction, not with those big ears she has."

Beatrice gathered up the other bags and headed for the house while Len grabbed his tools and equipment. Miss Sissy had dumped the bag on the dining room table, and Beatrice sighed again. There was really no point in putting everything away since it was time for them to eat. Food was generally a good distraction for Miss Sissy and the old woman was clearly in need of a distraction.

Beatrice lined up all the different options up on the table in a makeshift buffet and then laid out some plastic forks and knives, the napkins and paper plates. Miss Sissy sat on the sofa, watching her, her arms crossed defensively in front of her as Len plugged in a drill on a long cord.

Beatrice spotted the drill and said, "Miss Sissy, let's go ahead and fill our plates. Then we can take the food outside. It's about to get pretty loud in here."

Miss Sissy didn't need to be asked twice. Just a couple of minutes later, her paper plate was groaning with a loaded pimento cheese sandwich (Dappled Hills pimento cheese, of course), charcuteries, cheese, potato chips, pickles, and a ham sandwich. Beatrice wasn't even sure how the old woman found the room for the second sandwich on the plate. And she wasn't sure how Miss Sissy stayed as wiry as she was, despite her tremendous appetite.

Beatrice fixed a much more modest plate and then joined Miss Sissy in the backyard at the table.

Miss Sissy frowned at her. "Thought you were getting in the hammock," she muttered.

"Not to eat my food. I don't think I could lie down and eat if I tried. And I'm not sure that it's good for digestion to eat that way," said Beatrice. She hazarded a closer look at Miss Sissy. Beneath the gruff exterior, she could tell that she was upset. She really must have liked Salome, despite their fairly brief acquaintance. At least, she thought it was brief.

Beatrice decided to feel out whether the old woman wanted to talk about Salome or not. "How long have you known Salome?" she asked in a carefully casual voice. "Just since she started working at the Patchwork Cottage?"

Miss Sissy gave her a severe look and didn't deign to answer.

Beatrice continued, "It's just that I'm sorry that I didn't get to know her better than I did. I feel as if I'm supposed to know the entire congregation at church, but there's just no way. Or maybe there's just no way for *me*—I'm not as good at putting names with faces as I'd like to be. And Salome came to church fairly regularly, I think. I only really started to get to know her from the quilt shop, though."

Miss Sissy looked down at her plate. "Knew her from the shop," she said gruffly.

Beatrice said, "She knew a good deal about quilting, even though she wasn't in a guild."

Miss Sissy glared at her. "Didn't have time for a guild!"

"No, I suppose she didn't, not between a job and a daughter." She paused and looked at the old woman, who appeared very morose. Beatrice added gently, "If it makes you feel any better, I don't think that Salome even knew what happened. She wouldn't have suffered. And Ramsay is right on the trail of whoever did this."

Miss Sissy considered this and then nodded, her lips tightly held together. "Knew something," she muttered.

Beatrice's ears pricked up. "Knew something? Are you saying that Salome knew something? Something that may have led to her death?"

Miss Sissy glared again at the word *death*. "Heard her on the phone. Saying she saw somebody."

Beatrice leaned forward intently. "Did she say the person's name?"

Miss Sissy shook her head.

"Could you tell if she was talking to a man or a woman? Or if she knew them well or not?" asked Beatrice.

Miss Sissy shook her head again, this time regretfully.

Beatrice said, "It's all right. As I said, Ramsay will get to the bottom of this. At least this gives us a little insight into what might have happened."

The rest of the meal went much better. Miss Sissy offered some tidbits about Salome in her usual staccato delivery. Apparently, Salome had been very friendly with Maisie the shop cat, which had made Miss Sissy a tremendous fan of Salome's. Miss Sissy was part-owner of Maisie and hosted her at her house some of the time. Salome had fashioned a cat toy out of some feathers and string and Miss Sissy had loved watching Maisie scamper after the toy and bat at it.

After they finished eating, Beatrice said, "Okay. I'll throw away our plates and check on Len's progress. Then I think I'll read." She paused. She hadn't really considered how to entertain the old woman for the rest of the afternoon. Miss Sissy hadn't come over with a quilt project or anything. "I think I'll find my book and read for a while out here with you. Do you want a book to read?"

Miss Sissy glowered at her.

"Okay. Well, if you want to lie down, there's a spare room in the house."

"Not tired!" she said fiercely.

Beatrice sighed and walked inside. Len was completely focused on his work, which was refreshing. She'd sometimes seen the previous workmen on their various phones—not once or twice, which she totally understood, but many times and for long stretches. No wonder the kitchen hadn't been completed any faster.

Len finally glanced up, a good thing since Beatrice hadn't wanted to startle him. He gave her a thumbs-up sign. "Everything is looking good, Ms. Thompson."

Beatrice said, "That's a relief. I know that sometimes with these projects that you can get in there and then find *more* problems that need to be addressed."

Len paused. "Right. I didn't want to say this *immediately* because I know you've had such a hard time with this remodel, but there is one small issue.

He gestured to a long space on the wall, and Beatrice hurried over. "Is it water damage? Mold? This kitchen isn't exactly new."

"No ma'am, but it's probably something you want taken care of." He gestured again, and Beatrice peered closely at the backsplash over the counter, which is where he seemed to be pointing.

Her gaze combed over the tiles. "I'm afraid I don't see it," she said slowly, and then she stopped, making a face. "Oh heavens."

There was a gap between the top of the backsplash and the bottom of the cabinets that had been installed. In that gap, cement was visible.

Len said, "It's one of those things that you might not have immediately noticed, but would probably drive you crazy after a while."

Beatrice said ruefully, "You're right. And I have friends with eagle eyes who probably *would* have spotted it right away, and then I'd always see it whenever I walked into the kitchen. But what can we do about it? Remove the tile backsplash and start over?" She sincerely hoped not. That sounded expensive both in Len's time and their money.

He shook his head. "Nope. I'm thinking we just install a little bit of trim here and cover it up. Should work out fine. Of course, I'll have to run to the store to get some."

"Of course," said Beatrice.

Len hesitated and then said, "I also noticed one other thing. Sorry, but I figured you'd want to know right away when something didn't seem to be working that had already been put in."

Beatrice braced herself and nodded.

Len pulled a drawer with its new hardware. The drawer immediately bumped into the knob for one of the sink drawers and wouldn't fully open.

"This keeps the drawer from really being functional," he said with a shrug. "Again, it might not really bother you if you don't need the drawer."

Beatrice shook her head. "Our kitchen is so small that I need all the space we can get. I don't think that I can just stop using one of the drawers. Plus, won't it get damaged from bumping into the other drawer all the time?"

Len said, "Yes, ma'am. Especially if you yank it open to get a spatula out or something."

"What can we do about it? I can't even remember how it was set up originally," said Beatrice.

"I could remove the drawer and just have the cabinet underneath be especially tall. We can put shelving in there, and it could be a good place to put your pots and pans," he suggested.

Beatrice said, relieved, "Yes, let's do that. That makes more sense than having a drawer that can barely open." She paused. "I'm starting to think that I should leave you now. I don't think I can bear to hear anything else."

Len said in a soothing voice, "Running into issues is pretty normal. We can fix these things, and they won't be too expensive."

"Although they'll delay the process, I'm thinking."

Len nodded. "Afraid so. But not too long."

Beatrice said, "That's good. Thanks." She wandered off to find her book. But she didn't find it on her bedside table. She looked to see if it had maybe gotten under some things in the bedroom and then checked to see if she'd absently put it in a drawer. Nothing. She walked back into the living room and surveyed the whole area with her hands on her hips. The room was a disaster area, which was unusual. But the mess in the kitchen had caused everything to spill into the living room, which couldn't really handle the overflow. Beatrice started looking in piles of things until she finally found the book.

Before she could rejoin Miss Sissy in the backyard, her phone started ringing. She frowned, fishing it out of her pocket. She saw it was Piper.

Despite taking a deep, calming breath, her heart skipped a few beats. Piper, lately, had taken to texting her more than calling her. Could it be the baby?

"Piper?" she asked, her voice a little sharper than she wanted it to be.

"Hi, Mama," said Piper, sounding just a little breathless. "I just wanted to let you know that I'm fine, but I'm going to head to the doctor for a quick check."

Chapter Fourteen

"A quick check? Are you having contractions?" Beatrice fumbled, and her book fell to the floor. She absently picked it up, still focused on the phone call.

"Maybe. That is, it sort of *feels* like labor pains, but I just don't know for sure. Since it's regular office hours, I decided to just head over to the doctor's office instead of the hospital," said Piper.

"You're driving *yourself*?" asked Beatrice, now more concerned.

"I'm fine, really. I just wanted to make sure, that's all. The school called in a substitute, so I was able to leave."

"Where's Ash?" asked Beatrice. She was already looking around to see where she laid her car keys.

"His phone went to voice mail, which means he's in a meeting. But his meetings at school only last a few minutes, Mama, so he'll be checking in soon and will be on his way. Besides, it might even just be a false alarm." She paused. "It looks like Ash is trying to call me. I'll be in touch soon."

Piper rang off, and Beatrice took another deep breath. She answered quickly when the phone suddenly started ringing again. "Hello?"

It was Meadow, and she sounded wired. "Beatrice? Is everything okay? I just saw Piper drive by in the opposite direction. Why isn't she in school?"

Beatrice said in as calm and measured a voice as she could evoke, "Piper is just fine, Meadow. She's on her way to the doctor's office just to get a quick checkup."

"But she just *had* a checkup. What's changed?" Meadow's voice was both concerned and excited.

"She's having a few pains, and she wanted to get them checked out, that's all," said Beatrice. "She said it may be a false alarm, but she thought she'd go in to see since it was during office hours and she wouldn't have to go to the hospital."

Meadow was now really charged up. "So if they check her and say she's in labor, they'll need to transport her to the hospital. Where's Ash?"

"Piper thinks he's probably in a meeting."

"He didn't answer his *phone*?" demanded Meadow in a voice that seemed to indicate that Ash would live to regret that action.

"She said that his meetings are super-short and that he always checks his messages immediately afterward," said Beatrice.

"For heaven's *sake*," said Meadow in a disgusted voice. "Okay, here's what we'll do. I'll head over to their house and pick up the suitcase, just in case. They gave me a key in case of emergency. You go stay with Piper. After all, if she needs to go to the hospital all the way in Lenoir, she's going to need a ride. An ambulance from the doctor's office would be very expensive!"

"True," said Beatrice. "Except that I have Miss Sissy with me."

"Just grab her and take her along! When I meet you at the doctor's office with the luggage, I'll take Miss Sissy and you take the suitcase."

Beatrice opened her mouth to say something else, but then closed it again when she found that Meadow had already hung up. She had the feeling that Piper would consider Meadow's plan overkill, but it wouldn't hurt to be on the safe side in case Piper really *did* need to go to the hospital.

She walked out to the backyard. "Miss Sissy?"

The old woman, who'd apparently nodded off in her chair, jerked awake and glared at her.

"We're going to need to hop in the car."

Miss Sissy suddenly looked alert. "The baby?"

"We don't know yet. But I need to go to the doctor's office, just in case the baby's arriving. Meadow will meet us there later and can take you back to the Patchwork Cottage, if you like." Beatrice realized she'd have to text Wyatt to pick up Noo-noo, if she and Piper *did* need to head off to the hospital.

Miss Sissy galloped to the house, handbag clasped firmly to her side, looking fiercely proud to be part of an important moment. Beatrice hurried behind her, finally finding the car keys, and heading out the door, sending a quick text to Wyatt, just to keep him updated.

They climbed into Beatrice's car and set off.

"Poky!" growled Miss Sissy.

Beatrice thought she was pushing the speed limit a little, personally. Thank heavens Miss Sissy wasn't behind the wheel.

Otherwise, it would have meant a wild ride on the sidewalk to the doctor's office. "It's not an emergency," said Beatrice. "Piper is probably just fine."

Beatrice's phone started ringing persistently. It had fallen to the passenger's side floor in Beatrice's hurry to get into the car. "Can you get that?" Beatrice asked the old woman.

Miss Sissy, still looking very pleased to be part of all the action, reached down and snatched the phone up. She stared fiercely at the device, trying to decide how to answer it since her own phone was just a basic model. Finally figuring it out, she growled, "H'lo?" into the phone.

Then she grimaced and said, "Slow down!"

"I thought you said I was going too slow," muttered Beatrice, easing up on the accelerator a bit.

Miss Sissy frowned at her. "Not you, *her*," she said, gesturing to the phone.

"Here, put it on speaker," said Beatrice.

Miss Sissy looked at the phone suspiciously, through narrowed eyes.

"The microphone icon," said Beatrice.

Miss Sissy hit the right button and suddenly Meadow's voice filled the car. "Beatrice, it's a disaster! I can't get into their house."

A smile played at Beatrice's lips as she wondered briefly if Ash had wisely decided to change the locks. "What's wrong?"

Meadow sounded completely exasperated with herself, "Oh, I dropped the key down the storm drain in front of their house. Ugh! I just got too excited and fumbled it."

Beatrice said soothingly, "I think it's okay, Meadow. Ash will probably be on his way soon, and he can give us a key if we need to go grab Piper's suitcase. She won't need it right now. Just meet me over at the doctor's office."

Meadow sounded relieved. "Okay. Yes, you're right. I'll be right there!"

That's what Beatrice was worried about—Meadow endangering all her fellow motorists. "Take your time!" she said before Meadow hung up.

She parked in front of the doctor's office, and she and Miss Sissy hurried inside. The receptionist smiled at them: Beatrice looking rather flustered and Miss Sissy looking positively wild. "Can I help you?" she asked.

Just then the door from the back of the office opened up, and Piper walked out into the waiting room. "Mama? Miss Sissy?"

Miss Sissy demanded, "Where's the baby?"

Piper shook her head ruefully. "No baby today. Sorry for the false alarm. They were Braxton-Hicks contractions, that's all." She hugged them both, tightly. "Thanks so much for coming out, y'all."

Beatrice hugged her back. "No worries at all, sweetie. We just wanted to be here in case it was time." She pulled her phone out from her pocket. "I should call Meadow real quick with an update."

But there was no need as Meadow barreled into the doctor's office, eyes wide and chest heaving.

Piper hurried to her. "I'm fine, Meadow. The baby isn't on its way today. I'm sorry to get you so worried."

"Worried? No, I wasn't worried. Just excited," said Meadow, a tinge of disappointment in her voice. "But I can wait until our darling grandbaby is finally ready to come."

Piper said gently, "Sounds good. I'm going to head back to school to finish some things up. I've already texted Ash, too, and he's heading back to the university."

"That Ash," said Meadow darkly, as if the entire encounter between the key and the storm drain was his fault.

Piper hid a smile. "He was already getting in his car, Meadow, I promise. He called me back probably just eight minutes after I left the message."

Miss Sissy looked rather deflated but patted Piper on the arm. "Glad you're okay," she said gruffly. Piper gave her another hug.

A few minutes later, Beatrice and Miss Sissy were heading back to the house. Beatrice suddenly realized that they'd left Len completely unmonitored in their scramble to get out of the house. She checked in with him on his progress while Miss Sissy loped out to the backyard again.

Len had indeed made some progress on the work and updated her on it.

After checking in with Len, Beatrice fixed both herself and Miss Sissy some ice waters and headed for the backyard. She opened the door to find Miss Sissy sound asleep and snoring in the supposedly-hated hammock. Apparently, after a full tummy and a rather alarming day, Miss Sissy had decided to give the hammock a chance.

Beatrice settled in a chair at the table, but became uncomfortable after a little while. She was just contemplating a move into the living room, noise or no noise, when Wyatt came into the backyard.

He walked right up to her and gave her a tight hug. "I'm so glad you're all right."

Beatrice realized that it had been so busy after finding Salome that she hadn't even remembered to call Wyatt or text him and let him know what happened. All she'd had the presence of mind to do earlier was to text him about Piper and then to update him on Piper. "I'm sorry I didn't get in touch about Salome. It's been sort of a wild day. How did you find out?"

Wyatt said wryly, "Meadow called me a few minutes ago to update me on Piper and then launched into what happened to Salome. She'd heard from Ramsay, of course."

Beatrice sighed. "And I'd already given you a Piper update, although I was a total failure at updating you on what happened with Salome."

Wyatt said, "Do you know anything about what happened? I know it must have been such a shock to find her—I know how I felt when I found Gerald." There were grim lines on his face as he looked at her.

"It *was* awful—mostly because she was young and has a child and because I knew and liked her so much. The only good thing that I can say about her death is that I don't think she must have suffered. She was hit on the back of the head with a pan and likely never saw it coming," said Beatrice sadly. "She must have turned her back on the person who attacked her."

Wyatt shook his head, and they were quiet for a few moments.

Beatrice added, "And no, I don't really know what happened. All I can guess is that the person who murdered Gerald thought that Salome knew too much and decided that she had to be silenced."

Wyatt said, "But how would Salome know anything? It seems to me that she's been over at the Patchwork Cottage all the time. Or, if she's not there, that she was at home with her daughter."

"Yes, but Salome was at Gerald's office early on the day that he died. According to Miss Sissy, Salome was talking on the phone with someone that she'd seen at the office the morning Gerald was murdered. She'd planned on speaking with him again about supporting her daughter. She'd approached him about support before, and he'd turned her down. Fortunately, she'd had Carla to help her out. But she wanted to talk to him again and try to reason with Gerald about providing support. She knew his work hours better than anyone and drove up to the factory early in the morning to see him first thing with no one there. She said that she ended up leaving, but she might have seen someone or something before she did. Maybe she didn't even realize what she'd seen until later. But it might have been enough for someone to murder her."

Wyatt said, "If Miss Sissy is right and Salome was calling the killer on the phone, shouldn't it be someone that she knew? Otherwise, how would she get the phone number?"

Beatrice said thoughtfully, "Good point. Although she likely had everyone's number who might be considered a suspect since she was Gerald's assistant for so long and might have made phone calls for him. But it could be that she more easily knew how to contact one of the family members."

"You spoke to Ramsay?" asked Wyatt.

"A little bit. Then I spoke to Joan. She was very upset."

Wyatt nodded. "It must have been a really rough day for her. She didn't seem herself when we had our meeting about her father's service. Of course, why would she be?"

"What was that like?" asked Beatrice. "I was thinking that Laura Carpenter might want to be in charge of all of the arrangements. And it didn't seem to me that she was a huge fan of Joan's."

Wyatt said, "The meeting was all right. But you're right: Laura was definitely in charge of every aspect of the service. Joan just kept shrugging as if she didn't want to make suggestions because it might mean having a conversation with Laura. And Mark seemed very distracted, as if his mind was somewhere completely different."

Beatrice raised an eyebrow. "Well, that *does* surprise me. I could see *Mark* wanting to be in control of the service, too. I'd think that Laura and Mark would butt heads through the entire process. After all, making sure the family image is intact seemed very important to him. He was worried about the effect his father's murder might have on the business."

Wyatt shook his head. "Something else was on his mind. He was very quiet and reserved." He paused. "I'm a little scared to ask, but how is everything going inside?" He gestured to the house.

Beatrice said, "Len has made some good progress, but he also discovered some issues that are going to cause a few setbacks."

Wyatt chuckled. "I was afraid of that. When I was coming in, Len was on his way back out. He said something about going to the hardware store and that didn't sound like good news since we should have all the materials here."

Beatrice sighed. "Should have, yes. But he came across two problems from the previous contractor. They're the kind of things that need to be fixed. I guess we ended up with a better contractor because he spotted the problems pretty quickly."

Miss Sissy gave a prodigious snore, and they exchanged a smile.

"And she hated the hammock and didn't want anything to do with it," said Beatrice, rolling her eyes.

"Everything changes when it's naptime," said Wyatt.

"Maybe when she wakes up, she'll be a little better," said Beatrice.

Wyatt knit his brows. "She's not doing well?"

"She had made friends with Salome and was upset when she found out the news," said Beatrice.

"Upset in what way?"

"Angry. Which is Miss Sissy's favorite reaction to just about anything. Apparently, she'd gotten to know Salome while she was at the Patchwork Cottage. Anyway, we went to the grocery store for food and had a feast outside, which was a good distraction. And then Piper's false alarm created a *tremendous* distraction."

"And you're a good friend," said Wyatt, reaching out a hand for hers.

"Even though she drives me crazy sometimes," said Beatrice with a sigh. "When she wakes up, let's see if she's ready to head back to her house. I can't think of anything else to entertain her. And when Len is done for the day, I'll pick up Noo-noo."

Chapter Fifteen

Miss Sissy did wake up in a far better mood than she'd been in when she fell asleep. With a full stomach and a nap behind her, she was ready to go back home. And Len wrapped up for the day just a couple of hours after that.

The next couple of days went by much quieter than the previous ones. Len made quick progress in the house and Noo-noo made lots of quilting friends at the Patchwork Cottage. Beatrice finished up her work on the diaper bag and brought it over for Piper and they ate ice cream together (something Piper had been craving lately and which Beatrice was happy to indulge in, herself).

The morning of Gerald's funeral dawned rainy.

Beatrice looked out the bedroom window at the unrelenting rain. "This looks like the kind of day that Hollywood would create for a funeral."

Wyatt carefully tied his tie in the bedroom mirror. "I don't think Hollywood would make quite *this* much rain happen."

"You're right. It's like cats and dogs out there. At least Laura didn't want a graveside service, although it might be tricky even running into the sanctuary from the parking lot," said Beatrice.

"Do you know anything about this reception that's happening afterwards?"

Wyatt nodded and followed Beatrice into the living room. "Laura wanted everyone to come by their house. And it's certainly large enough to hold the number of people who are probably going to attend."

Beatrice said, "Unfortunately, any mention of an open gathering in Dappled Hills and the entire town shows up. Hopefully, Laura won't be totally overwhelmed."

A few minutes later, they headed to the church. There was no break in the clouds so they used large umbrellas and wore rain coats and sloshed through the puddles.

They were early, of course, with Wyatt officiating, and the church was already starting to fill up. Beatrice found a spot in the first third of the pews and spoke to a few members of the congregation as they came in.

She stood up to greet Mark Carpenter as he approached her. His mouth was set in a grim line, and he looked stressed. But then, it was his father's funeral. He sat down in front of her in a pew and turned around. "I heard that you found Salome Hewitt the other day." He spoke in a hushed voice although there was no one around them.

Beatrice nodded.

Mark sighed and rubbed his forehead with his hand. "I'm trying to get some more information on what happened and how things are going now with Salome's sister and daughter. I feel a sense of responsibility." He saw Beatrice looking curiously at him and quickly added, "As a former employer. Salome worked many years at Dappled Hills Pimento Cheese, and I want to make sure to recognize that."

"That's kind of you, especially considering that she hadn't been an employee there for a little while," said Beatrice.

Mark's neck flushed red. "My father and I didn't always see eye to eye when it came to the business. That was one instance in which we disagreed. I felt as if Salome had been a loyal employee for many years and was one of the few people who was as organized as my father was. I don't think he realized how good he had it until he went through a slew of replacements recently for Salome after he fired her."

There was no mention of the reason Salome had been fired, which made Beatrice wonder if Mark even knew.

"Anyway, I feel terrible about it. I contacted Ramsay just as soon as I heard that morning. I was in the office early, trying to get caught up, when one of our employees told me." He watched as more people filed into the church. "I feel terrible about it," he repeated in a somewhat automatic tone.

Beatrice said, "It's a tragedy, to be sure. I'm so glad that Salome's sister lives in town, for her daughter's sake."

Mark said, "I'm sure it's a comfort to Salome's child to have her aunt there."

Beatrice said, "And how are things for you? I'd imagine that it would be hard to try to step suddenly into your father's role."

Mark clearly didn't want to say anything that would make the business appear in a bad light. He said briskly, "Oh, it's been all right. Of course, I was very involved in the business anyway in terms of the general operation. There were a few areas, naturally, that my father liked to handle himself that could have been a challenge to step into. But the saving grace has been the fact that he was meticulously organized and made notes on everything that he did. I've gotten up to speed pretty quickly because I didn't want to let the employees down."

"How are things going with the employees? I'm sure that it must be so hard on everyone, having your father gone."

Mark appeared to be going off of a script when it came to the business. He quickly said, "Oh, the business is fit as a fiddle. It practically runs itself so it hasn't been too much of an adjustment. Everyone just does their job every day."

Beatrice nodded. "That's good. And I'm sure it must be helpful to have a routine right now. I know that's supposed to help when you're going through tough times."

Mark said, "It is, indeed. At least, for most people." His tone was dark, and he glanced around to make sure they couldn't be overheard. "Except, perhaps, for Laura. I noticed last night when I stopped by that she seemed to be busily packing her bags."

Beatrice stared at him. "Laura is getting ready to leave? For good or just a trip out of town to clear her head?"

Mark said dryly, "From the number of boxes I saw in the house, it certainly seemed to be for good." He added, "But you won't see them today, not with everyone at the house for the reception. She has everything upstairs packed up, though."

"Maybe she's having a hard time being in the same house now that your father is gone. I'd imagine that there would be constant reminders of him there. Could she be moving to another house locally?" asked Beatrice.

Mark shrugged. "I'm not sure, but I doubt it. Twice now, I've seen her hang a phone up hastily when I've entered the room. I strongly suspect that she's seeing someone else. And I'm not convinced that it hasn't been going on for a long time, either." He made a face. "Sorry. That's probably inappropriate, considering where we are. But it just made me angry when I saw it." He glanced up again at the people entering the church. "Being here in the church reminds me that I need to find the information Dad was working on: the bids for the church heating and air renovation. I'll take a look for those in the next few days."

"Thanks," said Beatrice. "It was nice of your father to do that for the church."

Mark gave a distracted nod. "I should go. Good talking to you, Beatrice."

Beatrice studied the church bulletin she'd been handed when I first came in. It looked like Laura, whatever her other failings might be, was definitely on top of things. She had managed, in a very short period of time, to reserve the best soloist in the church. There was also a string quartet and a brass section. From what she could see, it was going to be a celebration of Gerald's life instead of a more somber service.

She was interrupted by Meadow plopping down next to her. "Okay if I sit with you? Both of our hubbies are working this event, after all."

Beatrice turned and spotted Ramsay standing at the back of the sanctuary, keeping an eye on the large room. He lifted a hand in greeting.

Meadow made a face. "Once in a while, it would be nice to be able to actually sit with my husband. You must be used to it—sitting by yourself at church all the time."

Beatrice shrugged. "It's all right. I knew it would be that way going into the marriage. Besides, when I was single, I was sitting by myself, anyway."

Meadow said in her usual stage whisper, "Have you found anything out? About the murders, I mean?"

Beatrice chuckled. "Shouldn't you be asking Ramsay that? It's his case, after all. I'm sure he's found out some helpful information."

Meadow snorted. "Ramsay? You know how he is. He doesn't want me involved in it. He seems to be under the mistaken impression that I can't keep a secret."

"*Mistaken* impression?" asked Beatrice.

"You know that I can! Maybe not with *some* things, but with the most important stuff I can. And certainly when it comes to information about solving a murder. Besides, you're the one who found poor Salome. I think you have plenty of thoughts on what's going on. But all I can tell you is that Ramsay has been mostly focused on speaking with the family. I don't know if that's because he's hoping to widen the field of suspects by finding out if anyone outside the family had a grudge against Gerald or whether it's because he really thinks that a family member is responsible," said Meadow.

Beatrice made sure that no one was in earshot again. She was sure that, the way the church was filling up, someone would be next to them soon. "I've been speaking with the family members, too. I spoke to Mark just a few minutes ago, and he mentioned that Laura was packing up her things."

Meadow's mouth opened in an O. "No! Really? Is that because she just doesn't want to have lots of reminders of Gerald around? I mean, they were married for a while."

Beatrice said, "I asked Mark that, but he seemed to think that maybe Laura has another man."

"Wow. I can't imagine that Gerald would have been happy about that if he'd known about it," said Meadow frowning. "He doesn't seem like the kind of guy who would just look the other way if his wife was having an affair."

Beatrice said, "I guess we just never know what's going on in someone's marriage. But that was simply what Mark thought. Obviously, don't say anything to anyone about it."

"Aren't we going over to Laura's house right after this? Are we all to be sitting on boxes?"

Beatrice shook her head. "He said that she'd started packing up the upstairs so I don't think we'll even be able to tell that she's planning on moving when we're over there for the reception."

Meadow asked, "Have you spoken to anyone else again? I mean, since Salome died." She put her hand to her heart. "I simply cannot believe that we lost Salome. I'm really just heartbroken at that. And she had that little girl to raise! What a tragedy. It was so crazy that day with Piper heading to the doctor that I didn't even have a chance to ask you about it."

"It's very sad. I'm just relieved that Carla is in town and is so close to Salome's daughter. And I did—actually, I spoke to Joan right outside of Salome's house."

Meadow said, "Well, I'm not sure why Joan was outside Salome's house, but I'm sure she had absolutely nothing to do with it."

Beatrice said dryly, "Because she's a quilter?"

"Not just because she's a quilter! Because she absolutely thought that the sun rose and set in Salome. She was always saying how lucky her father was to have Salome helping him out. I think she was more furious with Gerald for letting Salome go than Salome was."

Beatrice asked in a low voice, "So another reason to hold Gerald responsible for something. She already blamed him for her mother's death."

"She just had a few issues with her father. I'm sure our children have a few issues with us, too—they're just too polite to voice them. That doesn't mean that Joan murdered her father."

Meadow's voice rose with her indignation level, and Beatrice made a hushing gesture. Meadow continued in a quieter voice, "What did Joan say?"

"At first, she was just shocked and upset, of course. As you mentioned, she was quite a fan of Salome's. She wasn't pointing fingers exactly, but she did bring up that Mark hasn't been acting like himself lately," said Beatrice.

"Well, of course he hasn't! His father was just murdered and now he's having to unexpectedly be responsible for an entire factory full of people," said Meadow. "What does she expect?"

"True, but I got the impression that it was more than that. Apparently, he's been very stressed and has been difficult to deal with lately. He's even been losing his temper at work, which Joan says is very unusual. And he hasn't been happy with Joan going over to the business, either."

Meadow frowned. "I didn't think that Joan was very interested in the factory."

"She's not—but she feels a responsibility to go over there and make sure everything is running smoothly with her father gone. And Mark hasn't wanted her to be there," said Beatrice.

Meadow shrugged. "Maybe Mark is trying to get the business ready to sell and he's not ready for anyone in the family to really know it yet. After all, he realized he was sort of on his own when he suggested that they sell it. He's probably trying to get everything set up, see what offers come in, and present it to the family."

"But my understanding is that Gerald left the factory to Mark. That means that he doesn't have to get support from the family to sell the business," said Beatrice.

"Maybe so, but it sure makes life a lot easier if he *does* get their approval," said Meadow. "Can you imagine what Christmases would be like if they were mad at him for selling?"

Beatrice said, "You're probably right. Although I have a feeling that the family wouldn't be opposed to a sale now that Gerald is gone. I think that one of the main reasons they were originally against it was because it was his entire life, and they wanted him to be happy, engaged, and out of trouble. Now that Gerald is dead, they may not really have a problem with the business being sold."

The organ music started soaring, and Beatrice and Meadow hastily turned toward the front and watched as Wyatt stepped out.

About halfway through the service, Meadow jabbed her with an elbow. Beatrice frowned at her, and Meadow loudly whispered, "Look behind you!"

Beatrice waited a discreet amount of time and then stretched to look casually behind her. She saw immediately who Meadow was referring to—it was Colleen. She was standing at the back of the church in an expensive suit in rather jaunty-looking colors that might have done better at a wedding than a funeral. She caught Beatrice's eye and gave her a wink. Beatrice smiled weakly and turned back around.

"Wonder what *she's* doing here?" asked Meadow.

Beatrice pressed her lips tightly together and shook her head. She had no desire to engage in a guessing game with Meadow right now, especially since it usually meant that Meadow would become louder and louder . . . something she didn't need in the middle of a funeral.

The service took slightly over an hour. Both of Gerald's children had briefly spoken and so had some of Gerald's friends from the church. Finally, one of Gerald's employees from the factory said a few words and had gotten quite choked up. Whatever else Gerald might have been, he did seem to have been a good employer.

After the service, Beatrice joined Wyatt at the front of the church to speak again with the family. A few members of the congregation gave their condolences, but it looked as if most of them were planning on speaking with the family at Laura's house. And, after about ten minutes, Mark and Joan left . . . Laura had left early to get home before anyone from the church arrived. Wyatt told Beatrice he needed to run to his office for a few minutes to make a few phone calls before heading to the reception.

Beatrice was gathering her purse when she heard her name. She glanced up to see Colleen standing there.

Chapter Sixteen

"Has Wyatt already left?" she frowned, looking around her.

"Not yet, but he's making a few calls. Is there something that I can help you with?" asked Beatrice.

Colleen sighed. "I'm not sure. Do you think he has any time either today or tomorrow to speak with me again about the wedding plans? I wanted to check and see how flexible the church was on some of the décor issues. If it made a difference, I could make a sizeable donation to the church. We just want things a particular way, that's all."

Beatrice gave her a tight smile. "I'll be happy to ask him to get in touch with you for a good date and time."

Colleen gave her a return smile, but she was already looking at the door. "Okay. Just see if you can tell him that it's important that we talk as soon as possible."

Colleen started moving toward the door, and Beatrice quickly said, "I'll do that. We've just had a lot going on lately. You may not have heard, but there was another tragic death here yesterday. I'm sure that Wyatt will be speaking with the family soon regarding a service. You may have known her, since you knew Gerald. Salome Hewitt?"

Colleen stiffened a little and then relaxed. "Salome Hewitt? The name doesn't ring a bell, I'm afraid. Who is she?"

"She was a long-time employee of Gerald's," said Beatrice. "I thought you might have heard about her death if you were in town yesterday morning. Dappled Hills has been talking about it a lot."

Colleen raised an eyebrow. "I can only imagine how much chatter goes on in a small town like Dappled Hills. Unfortunately, I *wasn't* here yesterday morning. I'd been out late the night before and gave myself the opportunity to sleep in. Besides, I'm in Lenoir most of the time—it's this wedding that's made me travel over to Dappled Hills so much."

She made it sound as if Dappled Hills was a long way from Lenoir when, in fact, it was only ten minutes away. Beatrice said, "The town is speaking even more about it because poor Salome was murdered."

"*What?*" now Colleen looked aggrieved. "Look, what's going on in this town? I thought I was planning my daughter's wedding in this cute little enclave and the next thing I know, there are killers at every turn! The last thing that I need is for some sort of tragedy to happen on Elena's special day. What's going on with the local police? Can't they find any leads at all?"

"I believe the police are working under the assumption that the crimes are related," said Beatrice dryly. "I doubt there's a serial killer working his way through Dappled Hills."

"Serial killer or not, surely the police are trying to get to the bottom of it all. Or is it like so many small towns? Do you have a Podunk police department?" asked Colleen.

"Not at all," said Beatrice, managing to keep her cool. In fact, perhaps she was doing too good of a job keeping her cool because her voice was now frosty. "I'm sure they'll turn up a lead soon. Maybe they'll speak with *you*, since you knew Gerald so well."

Colleen gave a bored shrug of a shoulder and was looking toward the door again. "I did and I didn't. Besides, just because I knew Gerald doesn't mean that I'd know his employees. After all, I was going out of my way to make sure that his family and his office weren't aware of anything. Why would I meet his assistant? Although, as I mentioned, I'm sure that I probably saw her in the office once or twice."

Beatrice paused. "I don't think I mentioned that Salome was Gerald's assistant."

Colleen's face flushed, and she turned on the defensive. "Of course you did. You told me she was his assistant."

"No, I said that she was his long-term employee," said Beatrice levelly.

Colleen blew out an exasperated sigh. "Well, I suppose I assumed that meant she was his assistant. Or maybe Gerald mentioned her to me and I retained her name somewhere in my subconscious. All I can tell you is that I never met her and I don't know anything about her. I'm sorry she's dead, but that's the truth. Besides, if you or the police are looking for information, you're looking in the wrong direction."

"Where should we be looking?" asked Beatrice.

"At the family, of course! They were always squabbling about one thing or another."

Beatrice asked, "Any family member in particular?"

"I'd focus on that wife of his. She always looked as if butter wouldn't melt in her mouth and she was *oh-so* devoted to Gerald." Colleen snorted. "That was all just a façade."

Beatrice asked, "You mean that they didn't have such a close relationship?"

Colleen said, "Let's just say that Laura should be on the stage. Really. She could act like the adoring wife to Gerald and then the next thing you know, she's hanging out with her boyfriend. And I use the term *boy*friend on purpose. That guy must have been about twenty-five."

Beatrice frowned. "How did you know about them?"

"Because they seem to think that if they drive all the way over to Lenoir that no one will know about their relationship! Ridiculous, but then I don't think that Laura has a whit of common sense. I saw the two of them on more than one occasion, canoodling at restaurants or at the park. Like I said, they seemed to think that they were in Europe or something and that no one in Dappled Hills would ever find out." Colleen rolled her eyes.

"Do you think the relationship was serious? On Laura's side, I mean?" asked Beatrice.

"I think that *Laura* thinks it is. I wouldn't be at all surprised if she's packing up her bags right now and getting ready to elope. The merry widow indeed," said Colleen with a sniff.

Beatrice paused. "Do you know if Laura benefits from Gerald's will?"

"If you're asking whether I think that Laura could have killed him to get a pot of money and freedom to run off with her young man, I absolutely do. Because Gerald, for all his faults, was a very traditional man. No prenup for him, and he certainly wouldn't have written her out of his will. Of *course* he left Laura money to provide for her," said Colleen.

"So Gerald didn't know anything about their relationship," mused Beatrice. She added, "Because surely he wouldn't have left Laura anything if he knew that he was being cheated on."

Colleen just smirked at her. "I don't know. I mean, wouldn't that be a great motive for murdering somebody? What if your Mr. Moneybags husband found out that you'd been having an affair? What if he felt very foolish and decided to divorce you and cut you out of his will? It seems to me that that would be a fantastic reason to murder him before he could do either one of those things. As I mentioned, they didn't have a prenuptial agreement, so Laura sure wouldn't want to be divorced if she were at fault."

Beatrice's eyes opened a little wider. "Are you saying that's what you think happened? That Laura murdered her husband when he discovered she was having an affair?"

Colleen gave that careless shrug. "Who knows? I don't. I'm just guessing. It sure sounds like it makes sense to me. And even if Gerald and his kids didn't get along super-well all the time, I still find it hard to believe that Mark or Joan would *kill* him over differences of opinion. They're his flesh and blood. But Laura might have."

Colleen glanced at her diamond-encrusted watch. "Okay, I've got to run. I sort of thought Wyatt would have wrapped up his phone calls by now, but whatever. You'll give him the message for me?"

And she was gone, heels clicking as she went on the stone floor.

Wyatt did return a few minutes later, apologizing as he came. "Sorry about that. I should have known that one of my calls should have been pushed back until after the reception. It's Emily Tanner—she's just been hospitalized, and I wanted to check in with her. But she can be occasionally . . ." He paused to find a kind phrasing.

Beatrice said, "Chatty. And don't worry about it. I was just speaking with Colleen Roberts."

Wyatt gave a small grimace. "Sorry to have you field that. Did she attend the funeral?"

"She did, or at least some of it. She was standing at the back," said Beatrice.

"Weren't there plenty of seats left in the pews?" asked Wyatt with a frown. "Otherwise, the ushers would have brought in a few chairs."

"I think she could have squeezed in somewhere." Wyatt was still frowning, and Beatrice reached out and squeezed his hand. "Don't worry; she wasn't neglected. She might have wanted to stand for some reason. Maybe she needed to stretch her legs or wasn't sure if she wanted to stay the entire time." An unkinder part of Beatrice silently suggested that perhaps Colleen didn't mind showing off a little bit in her fine clothes.

"Did she need anything?" asked Wyatt. "When you spoke with her?"

Beatrice sighed. "She wants to speak with you as soon as possible. Apparently, she wants to see how flexible the church rules are regarding décor."

Wyatt sighed, too. "All right. Well, I'll just have to explain the church's position on that again. I'll try to get in touch with her after the reception."

The reception was just as elaborate as the service had been. Laura had pulled out their finest silver, and there were crystal vases full of bouquets. The food was in silver chaffing dishes that certainly hadn't come from the church. In fact, Evelyn, one of the church ladies, had told Beatrice in hushed tones that Laura had rebuffed the church meal ministry's offer to bring in food. Instead, she'd had it catered by a place in Lenoir. But she *had* accepted the offer of the church ladies to help with serving, which was why they were there.

As expected, Beatrice saw no evidence of packing downstairs. The catering company had brought in chairs. She and Wyatt ate a little, spoke with the family, and then spoke with various members of the congregation. Beatrice was relieved when Wyatt suggested they head back home.

They had just settled back home and were both seriously considering short naps when there was a tap at the door. Noonoo started barking and looking concerned. Beatrice said, "Why do I have the feeling that's Len?" Her cell phone started ringing, and she let it go to voice mail.

It was. And on the one hand, Beatrice was glad to see him because she wanted their kitchen project finished ASAP. But on the other hand, it had already been a hectic day, and she'd been looking forward to a little quiet time.

"I've only got a little over an hour between jobs," said Len. "Thought I'd run by here and do some work while I could."

"That would be great," said Beatrice, trying to inject some enthusiasm in her voice.

Wyatt said, "I might sit outside for a while and read. Are you going to take Noo-noo out?"

Beatrice nodded absently, pulling out her phone to check for a message. A few seconds later she said, "The message was from Piper."

Wyatt quickly asked, "Everything okay?"

"She's fine. She apparently just heard about Salome."

Wyatt said, "I thought you might have told her about that."

Beatrice made a face. "I didn't want to tell her. She tends to worry about me, and she has enough on her mind, as it is. I should have known she'd hear about it. Well, I *expected* her to hear about Salome, but I was hoping that she might not find out that I found her. I'll take Noo-noo over there for a visit and talk to Piper in person. That should help relieve her mind."

Beatrice put Noo-noo into the backseat, carefully buckling her doggy seatbelt that attached to her harness. Then she rolled the window down as she drove off, and Noo-noo happily stuck her head out to smell all the wonderful smells in the air.

When Piper greeted them at the door, she was flushed and a little uncomfortable-looking. But she smiled when she saw her mother and bent over as much as she could to gently pat Noo-noo.

Piper straightened up and said, "Would you like to take a walk with me around the neighborhood? A very *slow* walk? I've been so restless today and there isn't as much to do around the house . . . we're pretty much set for the baby now, thanks to the shower. I feel like I just need to *do* something. Or at least move around."

"Of course," said Beatrice quickly and the two women set off with Noo-noo matching their pace and walking sedately in front of them.

"Sorry I didn't tell you about Salome," said Beatrice in a somber voice. "I felt like that was the last thing you needed to have on your mind right now. But I should have known that you'd hear about it."

Piper gave her mother a hug. "It's okay. I was just worried about you when I heard. Are you all right? I feel so bad—both you *and* Wyatt have discovered victims of violent crimes this week."

Beatrice sighed. "It was a shock, for sure. I didn't expect to discover something that serious, but I did feel as if something was wrong. Posy had asked me to go over there because Salome didn't report to work. When I got there, the back door was unlocked and slightly open."

Piper frowned. "Were there signs of a break-in? Did someone force themselves in and then leave the door open on the way back out?"

Beatrice said in a reassuring voice, "There were absolutely no signs of a break-in. I think the general public is completely safe."

Piper gave a snort and said, "I love you, Mama, but you're taking this Protecting Piper thing a little too far. I promise you that I don't think there some sort of lunatic serial killer invading Bradley. These crimes have to be connected, don't they? It's too much of a coincidence that Gerald Carpenter and his longtime assistant would both be murdered in the same week."

Beatrice said, "Exactly. Maybe someone thought that Salome knew something about Gerald's murder and they wanted to get rid of her before she could say anything." She paused. "And the fact that there was no sign of a break-in means that Salome probably knew her killer and let her in the door."

Piper shuddered, despite the warm day. "The murderer must have been watching Salome's house, right? To make sure that Salome's sister and her daughter weren't there."

Beatrice said, "Or else they already knew Salome's routine—that she went to work after Carla left with Jenna. Then they'd just be sure to arrive after that point, after her sister's car was gone."

Piper said grimly, "Who do you think could be responsible for this? Have you heard anything from Ramsay about it?"

"Not much, but then he's been busy with the case," said Beatrice. "But the investigation seems to be focused on Gerald's personal life . . . his family and people who were close to him."

Piper made a face. "That's terrible. The people who should have loved him the most and wanted to protect him the most are the prime suspects. And poor Ramsay; I know he'd rather be at home reading literature and writing poetry or short stories or something."

Beatrice gave her a small smile. "Usually that's the case. But right now? Maybe he's happy to be out of the house a little."

Piper grinned at her. "You mean because Meadow is talking about the baby all the time? When she calls me or comes over, even *I* get tired about talking about the baby."

"How have you been feeling today?" asked Beatrice. She gave Piper a wink. "See, I want to know about the baby too, it's just that I'm being more circumspect about it."

Piper chuckled. "I'm feeling fine, just really restless. The baby's been super-active lately and seems to have his or her days and nights messed up. When I'm trying to sleep, that's when the baby's dancing around."

"Maybe the baby's ready to be born, too," said Beatrice with a smile. "I know he or she's going to be so special because you and Ash are such special people."

Piper reached out and gave her mother a quick hug as they slowly walked down the street with Noo-noo.

After their walk, Piper declared herself ready for a nap, and fortunately the baby was apparently napping, too. Beatrice headed back home and was relieved to see that Len was no longer there at the house. What was more, he'd also made quite a bit of progress in the hour since he'd arrived—or at least, it looked that way.

"I think the work was at the stage where he could move some things back," said Wyatt.

"I'm just excited to see the fridge back in the kitchen," said Beatrice. "That's progress, for sure, even if we can't use the stove yet."

They spent a few minutes admiring the now-empty area where the fridge had been taking up residence in their living room. Noo-noo decided to take a nap while the house was finally quiet.

Beatrice asked, "I'm sad to disturb the peace and quiet of this moment, but did you have a chance to phone Colleen Roberts back?"

Wyatt nodded. "Our conversation was fine and she was very civil. I just reminded myself that she is simply trying to have the nicest ceremony possible to celebrate her daughter's union with her husband-to-be."

Beatrice said wryly, "Well, that's a very generous way of looking at it. You're a good example for me, Wyatt Thompson."

He smiled at her, "That being said, I didn't bend any of the rules for her. After all, the rules are there for a reason—to prevent damage to the church, excessive cleaning bills, or even avoiding fire hazards."

"How did she take that?" asked Beatrice as she plopped down on the sofa and started feeling sleepy.

"All right," said Wyatt thoughtfully. "Almost as if she had expected my response. I had the feeling that she was planning on broaching the topic again so wasn't worried about temporarily letting the subject go."

Beatrice groaned. "She's like a bulldog. She won't give up. And, regardless of whether she has all the various decorative stuff she wants, the wedding is sure to be lovely. All the weddings in that church are beautiful because the sanctuary itself is so gorgeous. It doesn't need candles and decorations."

"I'm sure she'll come to that conclusion," said Wyatt cheerfully.

Beatrice wasn't so sure. Her trust in human nature wasn't quite as well-developed as Wyatt's was.

Wyatt said, "What should we do the rest of the afternoon?"

Beatrice said, "I don't know about you, but I'm thinking our books and the hammock."

"I'll bring some pillows," said Wyatt.

Chapter Seventeen

The next morning, Beatrice was pulling a few weeds in the bed in front of the house when her phone rang. It was one of the church ladies who'd helped at Gerald's funeral reception.

"I'm so sorry to ask this," she said, "But I've left something at Laura Carpenter's house yesterday. I was going to run by today, but my mother has fallen and broken her hip and I've had to drop everything. Is there any way that you could run by there? I wouldn't ask except for the fact that it's a pair of glasses. I take them on and off all day, and I guess I left them in the kitchen somewhere."

That was perfect because Beatrice needed a good excuse to speak with Laura again, and she'd already brought food over. "That's no problem at all," she said. "Would you like me to bring them by the hospital when I have them?"

The church lady blew out a sigh of relief. "Could you? I hate to ask you to do that because I'm all the way in Lenoir."

"I'm happy to do it," said Beatrice.

She gave Laura a quick call, and Laura told her to come on by. Twenty minutes later, Beatrice was there, and Laura was ushering her in.

Beatrice wasn't going to turn down the invitation but said, "I'm sorry to intrude like this. You must be exhausted after a long and emotional day like yesterday."

Laura said, "Oh, it's an odd thing, but I'm energized around other people. The service was exhausting, for sure, but the reception afterwards really helped me to recoup. I did have a tough time falling asleep last night, though, because I was hyped up from having company here."

She handed Beatrice the misplaced eyeglasses and then said, "In fact, I'd love to speak with you for a few minutes. I'm procrastinating doing something that I don't enjoy and having a conversation with you sounds like a nice way of putting things off." She gestured to the sofa.

Beatrice smiled and took a seat. "I'd love to stay and talk for a few minutes. Sometimes a distraction is a good thing."

Laura made a face. "In this case, it definitely is. I'm packing. Well, packing and also making piles of Gerald's things to give away. It's not the easiest or most fun thing in the world to do."

Beatrice managed to contrive to look surprised. "Oh, I didn't realize you were moving. Just moving to a different home in Dappled Hills? Or leaving town altogether?"

Laura sighed. "Leaving Dappled Hills altogether, I'm afraid. Gerald was really the only thing keeping me here." She quickly added in case Beatrice thought she was being rude, "That's not to say that Dappled Hills isn't a lovely town. But I haven't really done a good job establishing a friend base here. And, with Gerald gone, I don't feel as if I have anyone in my corner. I think it's just as well that I leave."

Beatrice innocently said, "I'm surprised that Gerald's children aren't persuading you to stay."

Laura gave her a rueful look. "Let's face it—I was too young and they were too old for me to be a real stepmother to them. And we're nothing alike, so we really couldn't become friends. It was always something of an awkward relationship, at the best of times. I don't think they'll be sorry to see me leave, especially now."

"What's different now?" asked Beatrice.

Laura looked down as she twisted her wedding ring on her finger. "Well, Gerald's will. I don't think that it was exactly what Mark and Joan were expecting. It's a pity because I always feel that there shouldn't be any surprises in wills. Everyone should know everything in advance because it's the living that have to pay the consequences when someone is disappointed."

"And someone was disappointed in this instance?" Beatrice asked.

"I'm afraid they both were. Neither of the children apparently thought that Gerald was going to settle as much money on me as he actually did. I guess they thought he'd just assign some decent amount to make sure that I could comfortably find a job or marry again. But instead, I came out rather well." Laura had a faint smug expression on her face.

"Are you in charge of the business, as well? The pimento cheese company?"

Laura swiftly shook her head. "Heavens, no. No, and I wouldn't want to be. I'd have no idea what I was doing. But if Mark sells the business, as it seems very likely that he will, then I'll profit from that, too. The unfortunate thing is that the whole thing has made Mark and Joan very put-out with me. In fact, Mark is consulting lawyers. He is considering contesting the will."

Beatrice shifted a bit uncomfortably. This was getting into very personal territory.

Laura said quickly, "Oh, please, let's talk it over. I'm sorry, it's just that I don't have many people to talk to here, and this is a way for me to sort it all out."

Beatrice nodded and said, "I don't think that a lawyer could possibly say that Gerald wasn't in his right mind when the will was made. Aside from that, I don't know how Mark would be able to proceed."

Beatrice said, "That may be. But the fact remains that the will is unchanged."

Laura looked a bit cheered at this before deflating a little again. "Regardless, I can't stick around town. The air feels poisonous right now to me. Besides, there's nothing really here for me now that Gerald is gone."

Beatrice sighed. "It's been hard in town lately. I suppose you must have heard about Salome."

Laura looked blankly at her.

Beatrice said, "Salome Hewitt?"

Again there was no sign of recognition on Laura's face. She tilted her head to one side as Noo-noo frequently did when she was trying to figure out what Beatrice was saying.

"Sorry, you might not have known her name," said Beatrice. "Salome Hewitt was Gerald's assistant."

Laura said, "Oh, his *assistant*. No, you're right, I never knew her name. I never really visited Gerald at the office. It was completely his domain, no matter what Mark thought." She sighed. "I suppose it's Mark's domain now. That thought is rather disturbing to me. What happened with Salome?"

"She was murdered," said Beatrice.

This seemed to shake Laura up a little. "No way! She couldn't possibly have. I mean, two murders in a week in a town like Dappled Hills? What on earth is the world coming to?"

Beatrice said, "The police seem to be operating on the belief that they're connected. The police haven't visited you to ask you anything about it?"

"No, why would they? Like I said, I didn't know anything about Gerald's life at the office. I never went there, and he didn't tell me much about work. If he ever even mentioned his secretary, he'd simply have said 'my assistant' and didn't name her. Was she working for Mark then? Since he took over from Gerald, of course?"

Laura really *didn't* seem to know very much about what transpired at the Dappled Hills Pimento Cheese company.

"Actually," said Beatrice, "Gerald had fired Salome some time ago. She'd been working at the quilt shop while she was looking for work."

Laura blinked at her. "She must have screwed something up. Sorry, I know that must sound insensitive. But Gerald was a total perfectionist and quite organized. Maybe Salome lost some paperwork or filed something in the wrong place. He could be quite unforgiving when it came to those types of errors."

Beatrice didn't mention the real reason that Gerald had fired Salome—because she was requesting child support. Apparently, or at least as far as Beatrice could tell, Laura didn't know anything about it.

"When did this happen?" asked Laura.

Beatrice told her and Laura said, "I'm sorry about that. I hate to hear that one of the employees was in such a bad situation. But again, I wouldn't have any information about that. When she was murdered, I was busy here at the house, packing. I have quite a bit of the upstairs finished at this point."

Beatrice nodded.

Laura said quickly, "Anyway, enough about me and my troubles. Tell me how things are going on your end. I know about your horrid kitchen renovation—Joan mentioned that one day. And I saw you talking with Colleen after the funeral . . . I had to run back to the church to get my purse. I'm sorry you had to deal with her." She made a face.

Beatrice said, "Oh, I didn't realize you knew her."

Laura cocked an eyebrow at Beatrice. "I don't really. She and Gerald did fundraising things together. She fancies herself some sort of a society person, if you can have high society in Lenoir. I avoid her whenever I can. Even her voice is like nails on a chalkboard to me."

Beatrice wasn't quite sure what to say to this, so she kept her mouth shut and gave a sympathetic nod.

Laura continued, "You must have noticed how bossy Colleen is. Hasn't she tried bulldozing you at the church? She sure looked as if she was trying to when I saw the two of you in conversation after the service."

Beatrice said ruefully, "You're right. She was trying to get her way. I gather that's not unusual."

Laura shrugged. "That's what Gerald said. I think she drove him crazy."

Beatrice glanced at her watch. "I'm sorry, I've kept you for longer than I should have. I know you're busy packing."

Laura gave her a wry smile. "As fast as I can. But I'm glad you came by. It was good to speak to somebody. I sure can't speak with the family, and I really don't have anyone close to me here."

Minutes later, Beatrice set off for Lenoir with the eyeglasses, despite the church lady's protestations, and hand-delivered them. Then she set off back for Dappled Hills.

She remembered that she had a library book in the backseat, needing to be returned. She'd planned on just dropping it in the drive-by box outside the library, but decided she needed a few minutes of peace and quiet. She parked and walked inside. Beatrice always loved the inside of the old library. It was warmly lit and the librarians were always friendly and ready with a book recommendation. There were pastels on the walls and lots of reading nooks. One wall near the periodicals had a large gas fireplace that ran in the winter.

Since Beatrice already had the novel she was reading with Wyatt, she headed to the periodicals to skim through a few. She raised her eyebrows and grinned when she saw Ramsay there. He gave her a sheepish smile.

"Not like I have anything else to do," he said with a chuckle.

"I'm the same way. I just wanted to escape for a few minutes," said Beatrice.

He grinned at her. "Now that I find hard to believe. You and Wyatt are like two peas in a pod. And now you've got a little grandbaby coming? Life sounds pretty good." He paused.

"At least, pretty good if you two stopped finding bodies all the time."

"Have you found out anything?" asked Beatrice.

He hesitated and Beatrice said, "I won't say a word. Promise."

"Oh, I know you won't. I think I've just gotten super-cautious because of Meadow. She cannot keep a secret to save her life! Here's the thing. We found some things in Salome's stuff." He sighed. "How well did you know Salome?"

"Not as well as I probably should have," said Beatrice.

"Now you're sounding more like Meadow," said Ramsay with a shake of his head. "She keeps saying that she feels terrible that Salome was struggling and that she really didn't know about it. It's the whole 'sisterhood of quilting' thing. The reason I ask, is because I just can't really see Salome as this cloak-and-dagger type of person."

Beatrice frowned. "Cloak-and-dagger? You mean she was sneaking around over something?"

"It sure looks that way. Now, I know that Salome worked for Gerald for a long while and I know a little about how their relationship changed." He paused and cleared his throat. "I don't think that Gerald came off looking all that great."

"No, I don't, either."

"But the thing is that Salome had all these documents that it looks like she copied from the office. Even if she was *supposed* to have them in her possession at one point, she sure shouldn't have had them at her home and after she'd already lost her job," said Ramsay.

"What sorts of documents were these?" asked Beatrice.

"Well, it took us a while to sort through them, but they all appear to be instances in which Gerald made deposits to make the business's bottom line look better," said Ramsay.

Beatrice frowned. "You mean that Gerald may have been using his own money to supplement the business's income? But why would he have done something like that? From everything that I've heard, he had no intention of selling the factory."

Ramsay sighed. "Your guess is as good as mine. I think the guess I'm currently favoring is that Gerald was so proud of that company that he wanted to ensure the bottom line looked profitable, even if the business had some ups and downs. There was other evidence that he'd made the company look better than it did, too."

Beatrice said slowly, "I wonder if Mark knew that Gerald was siphoning personal funds to supplement the business?"

Ramsay shrugged. "Not sure. But my intuition tells me no. He'd have gotten into huge trouble if he'd sold the business, and then it was later discovered that it wasn't as profitable as Mark had made out."

"And those were the only documents that Salome had?" asked Beatrice. "She didn't just have a slew of papers from the office that she'd somehow forgotten to hand over?"

Ramsay shook his head. "The papers only pertained to this one matter. It wasn't as if she literally brought her work home every night, and there were lots of others. So we have to assume that Salome deliberately chose these damaging documents for a reason."

"To have some leverage. To try to make Gerald do what she needed him to do," said Beatrice.

"Or Mark," suggested Ramsay quietly. "Maybe she tried it twice. Maybe she approached Gerald before he died and asked him to lend support to her or else she'd disclose what she knew and leak the documents. Then, perhaps, when she didn't get anywhere and after Gerald's death, she thought Mark was a softer target."

"I don't know that I'd think that," said Beatrice. "Mark doesn't seem like any sort of a softie to me. He's all business, all the time, just like his father was."

"Then maybe she was simply desperate. Gerald didn't leave her anything in the will, of course, and Salome wasn't sure how she was going to support her daughter the way she wanted to. Maybe she set out to talk to Mark about it and push him to give her some sort of an allowance or a settlement," said Ramsay.

"Then he became upset and killed her," said Beatrice levelly. "Is that where you're going with this?"

Ramsay said, "It's a possibility. One of several that we're mulling over. But at least it's a development that we can pursue. Whoever this murderer is, he's done a good job of covering his tracks." He looked at Beatrice. "Have you found out anything on your end lately? I know you're good at sniffing out leads in a very innocuous way."

Beatrice gave a short laugh. "This time it seems as if everyone is spilling all their innermost thoughts to me. I believe it must be the Wyatt Effect."

Ramsay raised his eyebrows. "What's that?"

"Being married to a busy minister. I'm hearing all the things that Wyatt would be hearing, if Wyatt could be everywhere at once. I did just leave Laura Carpenter."

Ramsay said, "Still packing pretty fast?"

"She is. She called the environment 'poisonous' over there."

Ramsay blinked at her. "That's a new one on me. What on earth is so poisonous? Looks like a nice, big house. Gerald left her really comfortable, too."

"She meant the way that Gerald's children were treating her," said Beatrice.

Ramsay said, "Well, let's face it. She made out really well from the will, is probably seeing someone already, and is a suspect in a murder. I'm sure the kids aren't exactly delighted with her. That would make me feel uncomfortable, too."

"Laura said that Mark and Joan were contesting the will," said Beatrice.

"Yes, we've been following that pretty closely, as you can imagine. There's definitely some bad blood happening there. Oh, and Laura won't be leaving town until we're completely finished speaking with her . . . we've cautioned her about that," said Ramsay.

"That makes sense. I did speak with Mark before the service, and he didn't seem happy about the fact that Laura was leaving already. He thinks that she's already seeing someone, too."

Ramsay said, "That's who we got that information from. He said that she was hanging up the phone in a hurry when he walked into the room."

"The main impression that I got from Mark was that he wanted to make sure the business wasn't harmed at all. That the employees had a good transition from Gerald being at the helm to his being at the helm. And that the company wasn't harmed by the murder and the suspicion that's fallen on the family."

Ramsay said wryly, "Well, that's a tall order. We'll see how it goes. If we can go ahead and wrap up the case rapidly, though, he may have more of a shot at normalcy." He added, "Okay, enough of my work-talk. Tell me how your reading is going with Wyatt."

"Much better this time now that we're both reading fiction, like I told you. I think the fact that it's *historical* fiction makes it more interesting for Wyatt, too. The only problem is that I've gotten a little ahead of him now, and I have to wait for Wyatt to catch up so I won't inadvertently spoil the story for him," said Beatrice.

"I can't imagine you giving spoilers," said Ramsay. "Doesn't seem in character."

"They're accidental spoilers. Apparently, I'm a very animated reader," said Beatrice with a smile. "I'll gasp or laugh or say 'oh no.'"

"That's what years of living alone will do for you," said Ramsay with a laugh.

"Exactly, and now I have this terrible habit," said Beatrice. "I don't know if I'll be able to kick it, either, after decades of doing it. I didn't even realize that it was something I *did* until Wyatt pointed it out."

"Sounds like Wyatt has been keeping really busy."

"Just about as busy as you are," said Beatrice. "I know you've been swamped with these cases."

"Yes, but the difference is that I *want* to be swamped right now. Well, maybe not as much as I am today, but overall, it's a help to me. Otherwise, I'd be at home with Meadow. And Meadow, much as I love her, is getting more gaga over that baby every day. If I stayed at home, I think I'd go a little nuts."

"That's going to change just as soon as the baby's born," said Beatrice in a teasing tone. "Then Meadow will never be home because she'll be holding her grandbaby at Piper and Ash's house."

"Very true. And it's a day to look forward to," said Ramsay reverently.

Chapter Eighteen

After visiting with Ramsay at the library, Beatrice found a few magazines to read and was happily absorbed for the next forty-five minutes. Afterwards, she swung back by her house, which was mercifully quiet. Wyatt had texted her that Len was tied up that day but would be back the following day to work all day long. Wyatt was visiting church members who were in the hospital, running by the retirement home, and then working in his office at the church after that.

Noo-noo and Beatrice had just settled down in the hammock—Noo-noo, like Miss Sissy, had gotten rather partial to it after a period of being extremely suspicious of the device—when Noo-noo's ears perked up.

Beatrice groaned. "Did Len have a change of plans?" she muttered under her breath as Noo-noo looked toward the fence leading to the driveway.

But the voice that greeted her was decidedly un-Len-like. "Yoo-hoo! Beatrice? You here?"

It was Meadow. Beatrice groaned again but called back, "In the backyard. Come on back."

A moment later, Meadow appeared, a perky smile on her face. "Don't you and Noo-noo look so comfy? And with your book, too."

Beatrice managed a more gracious smile than she'd thought possible in response. "We thought we'd take a little break. There's no construction today, so it's nice and quiet."

Meadow said, "Well, I hate to disturb your reverie, but I've been scheming with Posy. I thought about calling you, but I'm just so restless with the baby coming that I can't sit still enough to finish a phone call. I thought I'd run by, instead."

Beatrice raised her eyebrows. "But you *didn't* run, did you? In this heat, I hope you drove."

"Silly." But then Meadow looked thoughtful. "Although, if I *had* run, maybe I would have gotten rid of some of that restlessness."

"Or you'd have alarmed motorists who aren't accustomed to seeing you run. They'd have thought you were having some sort of emergency," said Beatrice dryly. "Especially since you're not exactly wearing running gear."

Meadow looked down and chuckled at her flowing red top and black slacks. "I'd have terrorized the countryside."

Beatrice added, "And Meadow? Don't be so wound up about the baby. Piper is in the very best of hands. Everything is going to be just fine."

Meadow blew out at deep breath. "Oh, I know. It's just hard when something is very, very important to me, and I can't really help. And I don't really have any control over the situation at all. And then there was that false alarm. I just feel sort of helpless."

"But you *have* helped. You've helped prepare a lovely space for the baby. You've made some beautiful blankets. You've been a big help," said Beatrice.

Meadow looked doubtfully at her.

Beatrice continued, "And I can think of some ways that you could help Piper now, too, if you wanted to."

"I do want to," said Meadow with alacrity. "What is it? Every time I call her, she just says that she's fine and doesn't need anything. If you have a tip for something I can do besides climbing the walls, for heaven's sake give it to me! I've already volunteered for the church nursery once this week and am on the schedule for Sunday and it's still not enough to keep me occupied."

Beatrice said, "It's just that when I saw Piper yesterday, she seemed really uncomfortable."

"Back massages?" asked Meadow immediately.

Beatrice quickly shook her head. She was sure that was the very last thing that Piper wanted right now was for someone to be fussing over her. "No. I think she could use someone to run errands for her. Ash is doing a lot, of course, but he's working all the time, and it must be tough for him to be working *and* doing all the errands and things. Maybe trips to the grocery store or the drugstore? I'm sure she'd really appreciate that." Beatrice *hoped* she would appreciate it. Maybe it would just put Meadow more in Piper's proximity and drive her a little crazy in the process. But Piper seemed so uncomfortable that she'd imagine that little things might help out.

Meadow beamed at her. "That's *perfect*. I know Bub's grocery like the back of my hand. I can get her list, grab the stuff at the store, and put it away before she even realizes that I've done it."

"I know she'll appreciate it," said Beatrice, her fingers crossed outside of Meadow's view.

Meadow nodded and plopped down into one of the chairs facing the hammock. She said idly, "Who knew that babies could create so much stress?"

"Without even being born yet," said Beatrice with a smile.

"Exactly! I've been at my wit's end," said Meadow. She paused. "So, when you saw her yesterday, how did she seem?"

"A little out of sorts," said Beatrice, chuckling. "I think the heat and the baby weight were getting to her. She was uncomfortable, but was ready to take a very slow walk. I'm not even sure that our stroll was even fast enough or far enough for Noonoo to classify it as an actual walk."

Meadow's expression was hopeful. "Maybe that means that the baby is coming soon."

Beatrice said, "Or just that it's hot, and the baby is making her even hotter. She'll be fine."

They sat there for a few quiet moments, thinking about babies, being grandmothers, and when the baby might come.

Then Beatrice said, "Meadow, was there a particular reason that you dropped by?"

"Oh, mercy!" said Meadow, eyes open wide. "See what happens? As soon as I start talking about the baby, my brain simply doesn't operate any longer. I was coming here because Posy and I are about to go to Salome's house and see her sister and bring her some food. For heaven's sake. I can't seem to remember anything these days!"

Beatrice said, "Do I have time to run and pick something up from a restaurant or something? I'd been thinking that we should probably do something for Carla and Jenna."

"You definitely have time. Posy was waiting for her employee to get there and cover the shop for her. But we need to go ahead and set out because she's probably getting ready to leave in a few minutes."

There was nothing like going from a hammock with a corgi and a book to frantically trying to get ready for something you were already late for. A few minutes later, Beatrice hopped in Meadow's car, and they took off.

"Fried chicken would probably be good for them. Nothing too fancy because of Jenna," said Meadow. "Besides, we can pick that right up from the drive-through window."

"No vegetarians there, right?" asked Beatrice.

"Oh, pooh! You're right. Not the little girl, but Carla, the sister. I remembered for Posy and me, but forgot for you. Sorry," said Meadow.

"Something smells really good in the backseat," said Beatrice a little wistfully. She missed having cooked meals. She and Wyatt had been camping out in their house just a bit too long.

"Tomato pie," said Meadow. She turned to beam at her and turned the steering wheel at the same time, making Beatrice clutch the door. "And the tomatoes are gorgeous! Thick and meaty and juicy."

It was a good thing that Beatrice wasn't trying to compete. She ended up picking up a large fruit bowl at Bub's grocery. But the fruit was fresh and there was a nice variety of berries and melons.

"That'll end up making the perfect meal, along with Posy's big salad. And Posy is also bringing something for Salome's daughter to eat...homemade chicken nuggets or some such," said Meadow as they pulled to the curb in front of Salome's house. "Looks like Posy beat us here."

"No surprise there," said Beatrice dryly.

Posy walked up to Meadow's car with a wave. "Good to see you two," she said, giving them hugs. "I feel like things have been so crazy lately that I haven't had time for much of a real talk."

Meadow said impetuously, "Let's go to lunch together. Can we?"

Beatrice looked at her watch. "Has no one eaten? It's pretty late for lunch."

Posy said, "I haven't and I'm starving. Meadow, your tomato pie is making my stomach growl."

"Then it's a plan," said Meadow, grinning.

More solemnly, they walked up the front walk and tapped lightly on the door. Carla, Salome's sister, answered the door and gave them warm smiles. Her dark hair and dimples reminded Beatrice of Salome. "You're too sweet to come," she said. There was a tiredness in her eyes but she held the door open wide. "Can you come in for a few minutes?"

Beatrice said, "Just for a few. And we'll put this food away for you."

Salome's daughter looked shyly at them from the living room. Carla said gently, "Can you say thank you, Jenna?"

Jenna said, "Tank you!" making them all smile at her. It made Beatrice mist up a little that this little girl wouldn't grow up knowing her mother. Then Jenna popped off to play in her room as the women found spots in the fridge for the food in the small kitchen.

They sat down in the living room and Carla said, "You don't know how much I appreciate this. I feel as if I really don't know many people in town, since I've always spent most of my time working. It means a lot to have you come and bring food like this."

"It's our pleasure," said Posy warmly.

"How are you holding up?" asked Meadow with a furrowed brow.

Carla said with a sad smile, "Pretty well, under the circumstances." She looked at Beatrice. "Wyatt came by and helped me figure out what to do for a service for Salome. I decided, with everything going on right now, on a memorial service later, after things settle down. Salome's wishes were for cremation, so that's already been arranged." She gestured to a notebook on the coffee table. It was full of scribblings and figures.

Posy said, "You're so organized, Carla. I just wanted to let you know how very sorry I am about Salome. If there's anything that I can do to help out, please let me know."

Carla said, "Thank you. You've all done enough already. I think, right now, it's so busy with me trying to adjust. I'm just worried about *after* everything dies down. Then I think it'll be quiet here, and that's when it will all hit me."

Beatrice said, "You have childcare already for Jenna?"

Carla nodded. "That's right. It's actually the same program that she was with when Salome was . . . still with us. I thought that was important—for Jenna to continue with the program and the teachers that she was already used to. She's really such a great little girl that she's easy to take care of."

Meadow glanced toward the back of the house where they could hear Jenna talking quietly to her dolls. "Is Jenna doing all right?"

Carla sighed. "So far. At first, I wasn't really sure that she understood what was even going on. But at night, she's called out for Salome in her sleep a couple of times. That's been the hardest part."

Posy's eyes filled with tears. "The sweet little thing."

Carla said, "It's just all such a total shock. I don't understand how Salome could be gone. I mean, the whole year has just been so crazy. Ever since she lost her job, it's been one thing after another. But this is worse than I ever expected it could be." She smiled at Posy sadly. "We both really appreciated you giving her that job."

"I was delighted to try to help out, in a small way," said Posy.

Carla continued, almost to herself. "I mean, Salome was a pretty diplomatic person. When she spoke to Gerald, she told me what she said afterward. It was completely reasonable." She shook her head. "I'm sorry. Salome told you about Gerald, didn't she?"

The women nodded and Carla said, "Salome wasn't even being all that pushy about it. She just asked politely. And Gerald wouldn't listen to her. He wouldn't even keep her on at the company that she'd loyally served for so many years! I mean, it's one thing to deny child support. It's another to fire someone who's just asking you to be fair."

Beatrice asked slowly, "Did Salome try to ask him again? I mean, I know she was there the morning that Gerald was murdered, but I wondered if she was there another time to ask him again. After all, Gerald had a legal responsibility to provide support for Jenna."

Carla said wryly, "He might have had a legal responsibility, but Salome would have had to go through the courts to get him to comply, and she didn't exactly have the money to do that."

"What a mess," said Posy sympathetically.

Meadow waved her hands around in agitation. "That's completely ridiculous. Gerald should have just felt bad enough about the whole business that he contributed support to Jenna. Or he should have simply looked at that adorable little girl of his and *wanted* to help out. How unfeeling of him! Couldn't Salome have done something to pressure him to contribute, even if it wasn't through the courts?"

Carla was quiet for a minute, and then she said quietly, "I think Salome did. And I wonder if that's what got her killed."

The other women were quiet and Carla continued, "I didn't want to say anything because I would hate for anyone to think badly of Salome."

"Impossible!" said Meadow and Posy and Beatrice murmured their agreement.

"You see, the police took away some papers when they were here searching the house. And then they asked me whether I'd known about them. I had, but I hadn't totally understood what Salome's plans for them were or I'd have tried to dissuade her.

When she was still working at Dappled Hills Pimento Cheese, she'd collected some papers to show that Gerald's business wasn't in as good financial shape as he'd always let on. I didn't listen to her very carefully, and I wish I had. She told me about it, but I was in the middle of something else, and I didn't give Salome all of my attention." Carla flushed.

"It happens," said Beatrice wryly. "I know Wyatt frequently tells me things that I can't really remember later."

Carla nodded. "I can only guess why she had those papers—to hold them over Gerald's head and threaten to expose the business's weaknesses if he didn't help support Jenna."

Beatrice asked, "Do you think that's why Salome was at the company the morning Gerald was found dead?"

Carla said, "Yes. Oh, I'd originally thought that maybe she'd gone back over there to try to reason with Gerald, but that didn't really make sense. After all, she'd already asked Gerald for help, and he'd already turned her down. Why else would she go over there and risk further humiliation unless she had something new to discuss with him? Of course, I knew she had nothing to do with Gerald's murder. Why would she? That wouldn't have been a smart way to get money out of Gerald, and it wasn't as if he provided for Jenna in his will."

Meadow said darkly, "I still can't believe he wouldn't give her *something*. How completely twisted that is."

Carla said, "As far as I'm aware, he didn't give her anything." She paused and then shook her head. "Posy, I suspect that maybe you were slipping Salome a little extra right before the end. You're such a kind and caring person that it sounded like something you might do."

Posy colored a little and said, "That's really sweet of you to think so, and I wish that I could claim to have been that generous, but I'm afraid I didn't provide Salome with anything other than her salary."

Carla looked thoughtful. "That's interesting. I know that Salome came into some money before she died. She wouldn't tell me about it, except to acknowledge that she was about to have a bit of cash to handle some of the expenses. Maybe I'm wrong and Gerald did give her a little something."

"Well, whatever he gave her, it wasn't enough," said Meadow with a scowl.

Posy's brow was crinkled with concern. "You were saying before that you thought that someone at the business knew that she might still talk about the company's financial problems, and they wanted to get Salome out of the way?"

Carla sighed. "I hate thinking this way, but the only thing that really makes sense is that someone in the *family* wanted the business to appear solid, financially. If the family wanted to sell the company, which is what I understood from Salome that they wanted to do, it's only natural that they wouldn't want word to get out that it wasn't as viable as it appeared." She shook her head. "Like I said, I hate thinking that way, but it certainly sounds like a motive for murder."

Chapter Nineteen

The women eventually moved on to other subjects before leaving Carla. They walked to their cars, and Posy said sadly, "What a tragedy. But Jenna is in such good hands with Carla. She seems really smart and caring."

Meadow said, "She is. But it sure shouldn't have to be this way." She glanced over at Beatrice. "What are you doing for the rest of the day?"

Beatrice said, "I think I should check in with Wyatt and see what he's juggling. Can you drop me back off at the house?"

"Sure. I'm going to see if Piper needs anything," said Meadow. "It makes me happy to think that I can help her out."

Beatrice decided that she should text Piper and encourage her to find something, anything for Meadow to do . . . as a kindness.

When Beatrice returned home, Wyatt looked relieved to see her. "It's one of those days when everything happens at one time. There's an impromptu meeting called by the elders over the Sunday school building heating and cooling system. Plus, Juliana Crompton has passed away and I need to check in on the family. We have two members who have just been checked into the hospital, are facing surgery, and are requesting visits this afternoon. And Colleen Roberts has called several times and gone to voice mail because I've been on the phone. She sounds as if she's about to detonate."

Beatrice said, "That's enough stuff to fill a whole week! What can I help out with?"

Wyatt shook his head. "Most of those things are things that I have to do, myself."

"How about the Colleen Roberts conversation? I've already spoken to her once. Maybe I can at least calm her down and put everything in context for her—that this has been a very busy day and you'll get back to her about the ceremony as soon as you can."

Wyatt said, "In her last message, she said that it was no longer convenient for her to come to Dappled Hills today, but she wanted to meet in person. I don't suppose you fancy a trip to Lenoir, do you?"

Beatrice grinned at him. "As it happens, I can probably make it to Lenoir on autopilot today. I've already been there this morning to return some mislaid eyeglasses to one of the church ladies."

Wyatt grimaced. "Maybe you can put Colleen off until tomorrow, then. That's a lot of driving. And it doesn't sound as if it will be a very upbeat trip. She's pretty upset and seems to think I'm avoiding her. And the volunteer wedding coordinator for the church is out of town right now."

"I'll take care of it," said Beatrice firmly. "After all, if I don't have anything to do the rest of the day, I'll sit around and fret over Piper, just like Meadow. And I really don't want to be as much of a basket-case as Meadow is right now."

Wyatt looked relieved. "If you could take on that one task, that would make a huge difference. Thank you."

A minute later, he set off to the church for the meeting with the elders.

Beatrice first tried calling Colleen, using the number Wyatt had left her. The phone rang for several rings, and then a cranky Colleen picked up. "Yes?" she said crossly. "Who is this?"

"It's Beatrice Thompson," she said coolly. "I'm sorry that Wyatt hasn't been able to call you back—it's been quite a day here, and he's tied up for the remainder of it. But I'd be happy to try and help you, or at least relay a message if it's anything that requires a decision."

"Well, it's about time," snapped Colleen. "Look, I can't talk about this on the phone because I want to show someone from the church in person the type of lighting I'm talking about bringing in for the wedding ceremony. It's quite innocuous and certainly not any sort of a fire hazard."

"Maybe you could send a picture of it to us?" asked Beatrice.

"No, I want someone to actually handle the lighting and take a look at it. I swear that it has all sorts of safety features and things. I left a message about this, but who knows if anyone was responsible enough to listen to it. I can't leave Lenoir now because I have meetings coming up, myself. I'm on several boards," she said in a haughty tone.

Beatrice gritted her teeth for a minute, but managed to say in a measured voice, "As I mentioned, Wyatt is completely unavailable the remainder of the day, but I would be happy to drive over to Lenoir and meet with you about the lighting."

"Are you allowed to make a *decision* about the lighting?"

"No. But I can relay exactly what you're thinking to the people who do make the decisions," replied Beatrice.

"Can you come here immediately? Because I don't want to progress with arranging this wedding at that church unless this gets approved," said Colleen shortly. "The candles will be *fine*. I want you to see them."

"I'll get in the car in the next five minutes," said Beatrice.

Colleen gave her the address, and Beatrice let Noo-noo out, fed her, and then climbed into her car. Colleen certainly did like getting her way. At this point, Beatrice suspected that the church would rather have her take the wedding somewhere else . . . if Colleen could even find an alternate location that was available at this late date.

But before she could leave her driveway, Beatrice's phone rang. She saw it was Len and groaned. There didn't seem to be much room in the day today for construction and poor Noo-noo was in the house alone.

She picked up the phone. "Hi, Len."

Len's voice was apologetic. "Hi there, Ms. Thompson. Listen, I'm sorry about this, but I'm not going to be able to come by today. There's a problem that's come up at this other job I'm working on."

Beatrice brightened, even though she knew she shouldn't be happy that the project would be no closer to resolution today. "Sorry to hear that," she said, unable to keep the smile from her voice.

Len said, "And that's not the only thing. I'm afraid I left one of my tools at your house and I'm going to be needing it in about an hour. Can I maybe run by?"

Beatrice said, "Actually, we're going to be gone for the next hour, both of us." She looked at the sky and saw that the weather was still ominous. "I don't really want to leave the house unlocked. I'd leave your tool outside, but it's looking like rain. I'm running out of the house now, but I told the person I'm meeting with that I'd be right there. Can I run the tool by your worksite as soon as I'm done?"

"That would be great, if you could."

"Which one is it?" asked Beatrice, hoping that she would be able to even recognize the thing among the motley assortment of tools that were in her kitchen.

"It's a demolition bar," said Len.

Beatrice frowned. "Sorry, you'll have to describe it a little more than that. I'm not sure what that is."

"It looks sort of like a big crowbar. You won't be able to miss it because it's about five feet long. I think I left it propped up against a wall in there. Sorry, it's probably going to be hard for you to handle," said Len.

"No problem—I'll grab it," said Beatrice, "See you soon, Len."

She hurried back into the house and picked up the bar which was just as unwieldly and heavy as it could possibly be. But, likely, very useful for ripping out cabinets and countertops. She put it in the backseat and then headed off for Colleen's.

Her phone rang halfway there, and she sighed. Instead of reaching for it while driving, she decided to let the call go to voicemail. But she did glance over to make sure it wasn't a call from Piper. Fortunately, it seemed to be from a number she didn't recognize.

Colleen's house was right on the cusp of a mountain and had a fantastic view. The house itself, however, really didn't seem to fit into the landscape around it or with the other houses in her neighborhood. It looked as if it belonged at Versailles. It had turrets, towers, gargoyles, and lots of huge windows.

Beatrice frowned, remembering that Edgenora at the church had said that Colleen was not exactly good about paying her bills, even stiffing the church. Had she sunk everything into this monstrous house, or was she just the type of person who procrastinated when it was time to make payments? How was she keeping up with her lifestyle?

Beatrice parked the car, took the keys out of the ignition, and reached for her phone to check the message.

"Hi," said the voice on her voice mail. "This is Mark Carpenter. I was wondering if I could run by your house a little later this afternoon." There was a pause. "Thank you."

Beatrice frowned. What was that about? She couldn't think of a reason why Mark would need to drop by the house. Could it have anything to do with their conversation at the funeral service? Maybe he'd thought of something else to do with Laura.

She shoved her phone in her pocket and glanced back again at the monstrous house in front of her. If this was how Colleen spent money, maybe she really *was* short on cash. What if Colleen had been planning on blackmailing Gerald? Threatening to tell Laura about their affair? That would have been an excellent way of getting money because Gerald, despite how his business was doing, seemed to have plenty of cash on hand. But then why would she kill Gerald if she was depending on him for blackmail payments? Could she really have been that furious that he dumped her?

Colleen had seemed to know a lot about Gerald's business. She knew how organized he kept everything and how carefully his files were maintained. She also seemed to know a lot about him on a personal level—that he was too traditional to have a prenup and that Gerald wouldn't have wanted Laura to leave him because he'd have had to sacrifice a lot of money in a divorce.

What if Colleen killed Gerald when he threatened to turn the tables on her and expose her as a blackmailer? What if Salome knew that Colleen had been there that morning? Salome had already shown a propensity to blackmail, from complete desperation. And Salome's sister said that she had recently expected to come into some cash. Maybe Salome thought that Colleen was going to pay her that day that she killed her, instead.

Beatrice's phone started ringing, and she reached absently for it. It was Ash.

"Piper's having some pains, and we're on our way to Lenoir to check them out," he said in a calm and level voice. "I just wanted to keep you updated. She thinks it's probably a false alarm again and definitely nothing to worry about."

Beatrice said, "I'm right here in Lenoir now, Ash, so I can meet you over there as soon as I'm done here." She grimaced, remembering that she was supposed to be returning the demolition bar to Len. She'd have to call him and see what he wanted her to do.

"If you're here, that would be great. But like I said, Piper thinks it's probably nothing. Maybe some Braxton-Hicks again," Ash said. "I did throw her bag in the car, though, just in case."

"I'll be there just as soon as I can," said Beatrice. She swiftly called Wyatt. "Ash called me...he's heading for the hospital because Piper may be in labor. I'm at Colleen's house, but I haven't met with her yet."

Wyatt said, "Don't worry about Colleen. I'll head over there now—both of the ladies at the hospital are having tests done this afternoon before their surgery, and we've arranged to put off visiting until tomorrow."

"That sounds perfect. I'll keep you updated," said Beatrice and hung up the phone.

Beatrice jumped at sudden movement at her car window and swung her head around to see Colleen glaring at her.

Colleen's eyes narrowed, and she yanked impatiently on Beatrice's door, pulling it open. "You could get out of the car, you know. We're not going to get very far with our meeting if you don't."

Beatrice said carefully, trying to keep her suspicions about Colleen from showing, "Actually, I've just heard that my daughter might be going into labor so I need to join her in the hospital."

She was about to add that Wyatt was on his way over, but stopped at Colleen's expression. There must have been something in Beatrice's manner that tipped Colleen off. Some general unease that Beatrice wasn't able to completely cover up.

Colleen narrowed her eyes and snapped, "You're not going anywhere." And she reached into the car and grabbed the keys out of Beatrice's lap.

Chapter Twenty

Beatrice swiftly got out of the car and took a step toward Colleen, who took a step backward.

"Give those back to me," said Beatrice in a steely voice. "You can't keep me from getting to that hospital."

Colleen said, "I want to talk to you. I saw your face. You know something, don't you?"

Beatrice lunged at Colleen, who backed off again with the keys.

Colleen ran a few yards away while Beatrice glared at her. She pulled her phone out of her pants pocket and started dialing for help. Colleen interrupted her by lunging at her and knocking the phone out of her hands.

Colleen repeated, "You *know* something. I could tell you were snooping around. You sure were asking a lot of questions."

Beatrice raised her eyebrows. "As I recall, I *wasn't* asking a lot of questions. You were offering a lot of information." She thought quickly. Wyatt said he was on his way and, being Wyatt, he probably left immediately, not wanting to waste any time. If she could keep Colleen talking, maybe he would arrive soon, and it would be two against one.

Colleen said, "I don't know what you're talking about. What kind of information?"

Beatrice said, "I thought it was very interesting that you knew so much about Gerald's personal life."

"Why wouldn't I? I was very involved in his personal life, as I think I told you," Colleen said, rolling her eyes.

"It's one thing to know information about what's going on with his close family members. But it's another to know that Gerald didn't have a prenup. And another," said Beatrice, trying to sound as sure as she possibly could, "to try and blackmail someone."

Colleen gave a short laugh but there was a shred of worry in her eyes now. "What on earth are you talking about?"

"I'm simply saying that you blackmailed Gerald. You knew he was in a vulnerable spot, and you tried to press your advantage," answered Beatrice.

Colleen snorted. She threw a hand back to indicate the huge house behind her and jeered, "Why do you think I need to blackmail anybody? I sure don't have to commit crimes to earn a little spending money. Don't you see where I'm living?"

Beatrice nodded and said in a quiet voice, "I see exactly where you're living. Where you're living is making me wonder if maybe you're over-mortgaged. I also understand that you haven't paid the church fee yet for your daughter's wedding."

Colleen rolled her eyes. "That's called being busy, not being stretched for cash."

Beatrice calmly continued as if there hadn't been an interruption. Wyatt should be there soon. "It makes me wonder if there are other, more important and pressing, bills that you haven't paid. That would explain why you felt you needed to resort to blackmail. I have the feeling, though, that Gerald wasn't one to be blackmailed. He didn't strike me as the kind of person who would take very kindly to it. He wouldn't have wanted to be a victim."

Colleen said, "Wait, back up. You haven't even told me what I was supposed to be blackmailing Gerald over. What kind of leverage could I possibly have had over him? Oh, hold on—you probably think that I was threatening to tell Laura about Gerald's and my affair."

Beatrice said, "If you told Laura about your affair, it would have given her good reason to legitimately ask for a divorce, as the wronged party. And, with no prenuptial agreement, as you pointed out, Laura would be able to make out like a bandit from any divorce settlement."

Colleen's voice was a little higher when next she spoke, which told Beatrice that she might be getting close to the truth. "And you think that Laura would have *wanted* to divorce Gerald? But everyone in town always thought that they were the perfect picture of a happy couple. That they were so good together."

Beatrice said, "In some ways, they *were* good together. I think they had a successful partnership. But Mark believes that Laura is also seeing someone else. She's certainly happy to leave Dappled Hills behind; she's been packing up since before the funeral. If you'd told Laura that Gerald was having an affair with you, she'd have quickly been talking to a lawyer. And Gerald, proud as he was, would have felt thoroughly humiliated at being left. Plus, he would have taken quite a financial hit."

Beatrice moved closer to Colleen, and Colleen took a few steps back.

Colleen said, "What you're saying doesn't even make any sense. If I *had* been blackmailing Gerald, I certainly wouldn't have wanted to kill him. That would have meant that I wouldn't have gotten any more money from him."

Beatrice said, "Oh, but as I pointed out, Gerald wouldn't have *wanted* to be blackmailed. He would have hated being embarrassed over his wife leaving him, and he would have hated losing money that could have gone back into his business. But he also wouldn't have wanted to be a victim. I think he point-blank refused to talk with you about it. What's more, he likely announced he was going to turn the tables on you by calling the police and reporting that you were attempting to extort him."

Colleen snorted. "I see. And then I just tied up Gerald with some rope I conveniently had on me?"

Beatrice was quiet for a couple of beats. "Well, you've just confirmed that you knew how Gerald was murdered. And that wasn't public knowledge."

Colleen froze, and her eyes grew so wide that Beatrice could see the whites of them. She lunged for Beatrice and shoved her backward, making her stumble back a few steps before recovering. Before Beatrice knew it, Colleen was in her car and thrusting the keys in the ignition.

Beatrice hurried toward her but Colleen had already put the car in drive and was heading toward her through the yard, a wild gleam in her eyes. Beatrice barely had time to scramble out of the way before the car flew past her. Colleen was clearly intent on mowing her down.

She ran to her phone, still lying on the ground, and called Ramsay, who picked up immediately. "Any news from Piper?" he asked urgently.

Beatrice gasped out, "She's having some labor pains, but it may be nothing. But Ramsay, Colleen is the killer. She's trying to run me down with my car." She gave him the address.

"I'm not far. Hang on," he said in a grim voice before ending the call.

Colleen, in her eagerness to try to run Beatrice down, was in the middle of her large yard and was now swinging the car around for another pass at her. Beatrice bolted for a grove of trees and stood in the middle of them, trying to catch her breath.

Colleen hit the accelerator again, and then the car screeched to a stop. Colleen stood on the accelerator, and the engine roared but the car didn't move.

Colleen was totally focused on revving the engine and trying to move past the stump. Beatrice jogged up to the car, pulled open the door to the backseat, and grabbed Len's demolition bar just as Colleen, in a panic, was climbing out.

"You're not going *anywhere*," snapped Beatrice, repeating what Colleen herself had said to her just minutes before. And Colleen sank back down in Beatrice's front seat as two cars, one with a siren screaming, sped down Colleen's driveway.

Chapter Twenty-One

Minutes later, Colleen was handcuffed and glowering out the window of a state police car.

Wyatt had an arm around Beatrice and gave her a small hug from time to time as if to ascertain that she really was there and all right. Ramsay was making notes in his notebook and fielding excited calls from Meadow.

But Beatrice's explanation of what had just transpired was temporarily delayed by a phone call from Piper.

"Mom? Are you okay?" she immediately asked.

"Absolutely fine, sweetheart. I was just momentarily delayed. How are *you*?" asked Beatrice as Ramsay and Wyatt watched intently.

Piper gave a gasping chuckle. "Well, I'm actually in labor this time. But the pains aren't close together at all, and the doctor thinks I'll be in the labor and delivery room most of the day. So no hurry."

"I'll get there just as soon as I can," said Beatrice quickly.

"A nurse is coming in, so I'll let you go. See you soon." And Piper hung up.

Ramsay said, "Regardless of how long her labor is, I know you want to be over there as soon as possible, Beatrice, so we'll make this as fast as we possibly can. Now, how did you figure out that Colleen was the one behind the murders?"

Beatrice rubbed her head. "It was really just a lot of circumstantial evidence and hearsay."

Ramsay said, "And that's all right, because not only have we already found some evidence in Colleen's very stately home, but she's already given us a brief confession. It's like she just suddenly deflated."

Beatrice said, "That's good to hear. Honestly, I was just here because of a church thing."

Wyatt sighed. "I should have been here instead of you."

Beatrice said, "You had no way of knowing what was going to happen. At the time, Colleen was simply an irritating person who was trying to bend the rules for wedding ceremonies."

Ramsay said, "So you drove up and what happened? I'm assuming that *you* didn't do that to your car." He gestured to Beatrice's sedan, which was perched on a low stump.

Beatrice made a face at the car. "I hope it's still drivable."

"A tow truck is on the way," said Wyatt.

Beatrice said, "And you're right, Ramsay, Colleen did that. I didn't originally go off-roading and park on a stump. When I arrived, I started thinking things over. Colleen has this huge house, and I was thinking what Edgenora had told me—that the church still hadn't received payment from her. I wondered if maybe Colleen was stretched, financially."

Ramsay nodded. "And we've found records to that effect inside her house. Also, we've seen that Colleen isn't very good about opening up her bills."

Beatrice said, "It makes sense. It's funny to think that apparently Colleen and Gerald met at a fundraising event. I suppose she was trying to project a particular image but just couldn't keep up with her lifestyle. That's why I started thinking about blackmail."

"What made you automatically consider that?" asked Ramsay. "Wouldn't it have been more natural for someone like Colleen to instead just move to a smaller house and curtail some of her expenses?"

"It would have been more natural, but it wouldn't have been *Colleen*. I've seen every indication that Colleen loves her lifestyle and wants to keep it up. Colleen also shared some very interesting inside information about Gerald and Laura's marriage. She referred to the fact that they didn't have a prenuptial agreement."

Wyatt frowned. "So a dissolution of their marriage would mean that Laura might be entitled to a great deal of money."

Ramsay gave a low whistle. "And Gerald was using a lot of money to fund his business during bad months."

"Exactly," said Beatrice. "And Joan, one of the times I'd spoken with her, called her father a 'proud man' and said that he would have hated any 'public humiliation'. Gerald wouldn't have been pleased about his wife leaving him."

Wyatt said, "So, at some point, Colleen started blackmailing Gerald."

Beatrice said, "Actually, she didn't. But she *thought* she would be blackmailing him."

Wyatt said, "Okay. So she approached Gerald and told him that she was going to tell Laura about their affair. Colleen believed that Gerald would pay her money to keep the information quiet—he wouldn't want Laura to divorce him because he stood to lose a good deal of money in the process and needed it for Dappled Hills Pimento Cheese."

"Exactly," said Beatrice.

"But Gerald didn't allow himself to be blackmailed? How did he end up murdered?" asked Wyatt.

Beatrice glanced over at Ramsay who cleared his throat. "Yes. Well, according to Colleen, Gerald not only refused to be blackmailed, but he threatened to tell the police, regardless of the outcome. He mentioned that he had a meeting at the church that I'd be attending the next day and would tell me then."

Wyatt nodded, "That's right. You were both on the church budget committee."

"Exactly. So in Gerald's mind, he'd see me at the meeting and tip me off. Apparently, after he told Colleen that, he really told her off—called her names, said mean-spirited things about their former relationship, that type of thing. She was also still angry at him for breaking up with her publicly. Pride played a big role in Gerald's death."

Beatrice said, "Colleen might have thought of Gerald as being proud, but she was exactly the same way. It must have infuriated her when he said those things to her."

Ramsay nodded. "The thing was, she was also very familiar with his office because that's where they would frequently meet before work or over the weekend, whenever no one was around. She knew that Gerald had a collection of unused sleeping pills there. She also knew Gerald's habits—that he was the first one over at the office every day and started out with a cup of black coffee. The following day, she returned to his office, put the pills in the coffee, and slipped back outside, waiting for him to drink it. When he became sufficiently woozy, Colleen went back inside and tied him up to prevent him from making any phone calls. Although, with the number of pills that she gave him, he wasn't going to wake up."

Beatrice said, "So that explains Gerald's death. At least, it's as much of an explanation as we're going to get."

"And Salome?" asked Wyatt.

Ramsay sighed. "I think she was in the wrong place at the wrong time."

Beatrice said, "*Was* Salome outside when Colleen killed Gerald? I know that she wanted to talk to Gerald and ask him for child support. And was likely going to blackmail him for it."

Ramsay said, "According to Colleen, Salome wasn't outside then, no. But she was outside the day before when Colleen tried to blackmail Gerald. From what I'm guessing, Salome was still in the process of collecting some more incriminating documents to use against Gerald, if needed. She saw Colleen storm out of the office. And Salome, being Gerald's assistant, knew exactly who Colleen was. At some point, Salome put two and two together and got in touch with Colleen, hoping she would pay her off. Although I don't know how she got Colleen's contact information."

Beatrice said, "Salome told me that she'd been at the office for so long that she still had all of Gerald's contacts on her phone. Almost as if she expected him to ask her to call someone for him, she said."

Wyatt said, "And when Colleen heard from Salome, Colleen killed her to keep her quiet."

Ramsay nodded. "She waited until Salome was alone and then attacked her with the frying pan."

Wyatt shook his head. "I can't believe that she thought she'd get away with it."

Ramsay said, "Not only did she think she'd get away with it, but she was determined to keep anyone from finding out. Clearly, that's what happened with Beatrice. Colleen realized that Beatrice was suspicious, wasn't sure exactly what she knew, and decided to ensure that she'd stay silent. For good."

Beatrice gave a wry smile. "And then found her plans curtailed. She did try to send me off in the wrong direction by telling me about Laura's affair—she'd apparently seen Laura and her friend in Lenoir a few times. But Colleen would never have told Gerald about it because it would have foiled her blackmail plan if Gerald had realized he wasn't the only unfaithful partner in the marriage."

The tow truck pulled into the driveway, and Ramsay gestured to Beatrice's car.

As the driver worked to remove the car from the stump, Beatrice said, "Wyatt, I have a couple of loose ends from this crazy day. First off, Mark Carpenter called and said he wanted to stop by the house. Any idea what that might be about?"

Wyatt nodded. "He called me back when he couldn't reach you. He just found the bid information for the church's heating and air conditioning project and wanted to make sure we got it."

"Oh, okay, got it. The other thing is that Len apparently really needs this demolition bar that I was using to ward off Colleen. I'd promised to bring it over to the house he's working on, but I think my plans have changed," said Beatrice with a laugh.

Wyatt said, "I'll call him back and see if he still needs it today."

A few minutes later, the car was free and apparently none the worse from the experience. Beatrice hopped in.

Wyatt said, "I'll meet you at the hospital as soon as I can. Len says that he does still need the bar, so I'll run it over to him really quickly."

Ramsay sighed, looking at Colleen still staring out of the police car window. "I'll be there as soon as I can, but I have some loose ends to take care of. I've no doubt that Meadow is already there or on her way."

As it happened, Piper's labor didn't end up being as long and protracted as the doctor had originally thought. When Beatrice arrived at the hospital, she was just in time to hold one of Piper's hands as Ash gripped Piper's other and a lustily-crying baby boy arrived. When a teary-eyed but ecstatic Meadow arrived (she'd left a dental appointment halfway through a cleaning), she was greeted by a beaming Ash and the beautiful little boy he held in his arms.

Ash then carefully gave the baby back to Piper.

Piper gave them a tired smile and asked, "Cutest baby ever?"

"And then some!" said Meadow as happy tears streamed down her cheeks.

Ash asked Piper, "Should we tell them?"

Piper's eyes crinkled in a smile. "You tell them."

Ash said, "We're calling him William. Will, for short."

Meadow said, "The cutest name ever!"

Beatrice said, "I think he has your eyes, Piper."

"And yours, too!" said Piper with a grin.

Beatrice added, "But Ash's dark hair."

Meadow said, "The perfect blending of both parents!"

The nurse came back in and said briskly, "There are a few things I need to do with Mom and baby—but I'll have him in the hospital nursery in just a few minutes if you'd like to watch through the glass."

This was clearly their signal to go, so they walked into the hall, Ash staying with Piper.

Meadow said, "What a happy day! I'm just so *glad* that Piper and little Will are doing so well. He is the most beautiful baby ever." She paused. "But where on earth is Ramsay? Has there been a development with the case?"

Beatrice glanced at Wyatt and then said, "It's probably not the best time to go over it all, but Ramsay is in the process of arresting Colleen Roberts."

"*What?*"

Beatrice gave her a short version of the story with just the headlines. She ended by saying, "But Ramsay said he'd be over as soon as he could."

Meadow's eyes narrowed. "That Colleen! She's the worst. Trying to spoil our special day with the baby. The very idea!"

Wyatt said, "But it didn't work. And the good news is that it's all over, and we don't have to worry any longer about a dangerous person being on the loose."

Meadow nodded and somehow coaxed a smile out. "All we have to worry about is spoiling that little grandbaby."

Beatrice turned to see Ramsay hurrying toward them with a large stuffed bear from the hospital gift shop. She grinned. "Somehow I don't think that spoiling the baby is going to be a problem."

About the Author:

Elizabeth writes the Southern Quilting mysteries and Memphis Barbeque mysteries for Penguin Random House and the Myrtle Clover series for Midnight Ink and independently. She blogs at ElizabethSpannCraig.com/blog, named by Writer's Digest as one of the 101 Best Websites for Writers. Elizabeth makes her home in Matthews, North Carolina, with her husband. She's the mother of two.

Sign up for Elizabeth's free newsletter to stay updated on releases:

https://elizabethspanncraig.com/newsletter/

This and That

I love hearing from my readers. You can find me on Facebook as Elizabeth Spann Craig Author, on Twitter as elizabethscraig, on my website at elizabethspanncraig.com, and by email at elizabethspanncraig@gmail.com.

Thanks so much for reading my book...I appreciate it. If you enjoyed the story, would you please leave a short review on the site where you purchased it? Just a few words would be great. Not only do I feel encouraged reading them, but they also help other readers discover my books. Thank you!

Did you know my books are available in print and ebook formats? And most of the Myrtle Clover series is available in audio. Find them on Audible or iTunes.

Interested in having a character named after you? In a preview of my books before they're released? Or even just your name listed in the acknowledgments of a future book? Visit my Patreon page at https://www.patreon.com/elizabethspanncraig.

I have Myrtle Clover tote bags, charms, magnets, and other goodies at my Café Press shop: https://www.cafepress.com/cozymystery

If you'd like an autographed book for yourself or a friend, please visit my Etsy page.

I'd also like to thank some folks who helped me put this book together. Thanks to my cover designer, Karri Klawiter, for her awesome covers. Thanks to my editor, Judy Beatty, for all of her help. Thanks to beta readers Amanda Arrieta and Dan Harris for all of their helpful suggestions and careful reading. Thanks, as always, to my family and readers.

Other Works by the Author:

Myrtle Clover Series in Order (be sure to look for the Myrtle series in audio, ebook, and print):

Pretty is as Pretty Dies

Progressive Dinner Deadly

A Dyeing Shame

A Body in the Backyard

Death at a Drop-In

A Body at Book Club

Death Pays a Visit

A Body at Bunco

Murder on Opening Night

Cruising for Murder

Cooking is Murder

A Body in the Trunk

Cleaning is Murder

Edit to Death

Hushed Up (late 2019)

Southern Quilting Mysteries in Order:

Quilt or Innocence

Knot What it Seams

Quilt Trip

Shear Trouble

Tying the Knot

Patch of Trouble

Fall to Pieces

Rest in Pieces

On Pins and Needles

Fit to be Tied

The Village Library Mysteries in Order (Debuting 2019):

Checked Out

Overdue (late 2019)

Memphis Barbeque Mysteries in Order (Written as Riley Adams):

Delicious and Suspicious

Finger Lickin' Dead

Hickory Smoked Homicide

Rubbed Out

And a standalone "cozy zombie" novel: Race to Refuge, written as Liz Craig